The Different Girl

GORDON DAHLQUIST

speak

An Imprint of Penguin Group (USA)

SPEAK
Published by the Penguin Group
Penguin Group (USA) LLC
375 Hudson Street
New York, New York 10014, U.S.A.

USA * Canada * UK * Ireland * Australia
New Zealand * India * South Africa * China

penguin.com
A Penguin Random House Company

First published in the United States of America by Dutton Books,
a member of Penguin Group (USA), 2013
Published by Speak, an imprint of Penguin Group (USA) LLC, 2014

THE LIBRARY OF CONGRESS HAS CATALOGED THE DUTTON BOOKS EDITION AS FOLLOWS:
Dahlquist, Gordon.
The different girl / Gordon Dahlquist.—1st ed.
p. cm.
Summary: "Veronika. Caroline. Isobel. Eleanor. One blond, one brunette, one redhead, one with
hair black as tar. Four otherwise identical girls who spend their days in sync, tasked to learn. But
when May, a very different kind of girl—the lone survivor of a recent shipwreck—suddenly and
mysteriously arrives on the island, an unsettling mirror is about to be held up to the life the girls
have never before questioned"—Provided by publisher.
ISBN 978-0-525-42597-7 (hardback)
[1. Science fiction. 2. Artificial intelligence—Fiction.] I. Title.
PZ7.D15164Dif 2013
[Fic]—dc23
2012024697

Speak ISBN 978-0-14-242365-3

Printed in the United States of America

1 3 5 7 9 10 8 6 4 2

For Anne

The
Different
Girl

1.

My name is Veronika. We had been there for years, but I only remember things from part of that time. Living on the island was like that, because it seemed to be always bright, and always hot, and every day passed like the day before. I'm telling this from afterward, from now, but I'm telling as much as I can remember. I hope what I'm telling is what really happened, because if it isn't—if I've forgotten things or lost them— then I've lost part of myself. I'm not sure how old I am, mainly because there are so many different ways to tell time—one way with clocks and watches and sunsets, or other ways with how many times a person laughs, or what they forget, or how they change their minds about what they care about, or why, or whom. And there are times when something happens that you don't understand—but somehow you still know that it's important—like walking through a door you only notice when you hear it lock behind.

I was one of four. The others were Isobel, Caroline, and Eleanor, and it was always easy to tell us apart because we each had different colored hair. Isobel's was yellow, like lemons. Caroline's was brown, like coconuts. Eleanor's was black as wet tar. My hair is the color of red rust. Aside from that we were all the same size and weight and age and always seemed to be doing, and wanting to do, almost always the exact thing as one another. We were all orphans, without family or even the memories of family, because we were too young when our parents died, which had all happened in the same terrible accident. Irene explained that we were on our island because the plane had crashed on one of the bigger islands, and everyone thought it would be better for the children to be placed nearby rather than sent away on another plane. Since all we knew about planes was that they crashed and killed people, and none of us had any real memories of our parents, and we all loved the island and Irene and even Robbert, we didn't want it any other way.

The island was small, but large enough to us. We lived in two buildings on stilts, so lizards and rats couldn't get in, even though they did anyway. We would chase the rats, and sometimes the lizards, but Irene explained that lizards ate bugs, so we really oughtn't chase them, but sometimes we chased them anyway, trying to make them throw their tails off. We collected tails.

We had a bedroom with cots and lockers. On the same floor was the kitchen and a room for storage. Upstairs was Irene's room, which had a foamy bed that bounced. Where we lived on the island, it was only from her roof that you could actually see the water.

The beach went around half of the island, and where it didn't there were steep and sharp black rocks, which were full of crabs. Also there were the woods, which is what we called a great meadow of palms and scrub and grass that grew almost as tall as us four. The woods covered most of the island except for the beach, the cleared courtyard where we lived, and the dock where the supply boat came. Neither Irene nor Robbert could swim, so none of us were taught to swim, either. We were allowed to walk on the beach, but never to go in.

Robbert's building had our classroom. The back room was where he lived, but it was mainly full of his different machines. If we asked to go back there, he would pretend that he hadn't heard us, especially if there was more than one of us asking. If I asked him by myself, he'd get an entirely different face on, for just a moment. Then he'd ask, "Do you know what kind of fish you find in the darkest blue water?"

When he said this—in a whisper—I would just shut up. Then

he would smile. I never knew if he wanted to confuse me, or if he was waiting for me to ask again, but because I didn't know I never did.

Irene took care of mostly everything. She was thicker and taller than we were, and she was strong. Her skin was sunburned, with a different texture, like another kind of smooth. She held her black hair back with clips. Once I pulled a white hair from her hairbrush and held it to the light. I didn't know you could have two different colors of hair. Irene and Robbert both wore white coats over whatever else, usually shorts and a shirt with buttons. Irene wore sandals. Robbert wore sneakers without socks. His hair was black, too, but he never went into the sun, so his skin was almost like a fish, except with blue veins. We all looked the same. We wore smocks with ties up the back, which we tied for one another, or Irene tied them for us, depending on what we were learning that day. None of us wore shoes.

Irene would wake us in the morning, one at a time. I don't remember dreams, so I would open my eyes like I had just shut them, except now it was day. The island's morning sounds were different from the evening sounds. In the morning there were gulls and little brown birds that lived in the palms. At night there were parrots, which are very loud, and crickets, which are even louder.

Caroline sometimes did remember dreams, or that's what

Irene called them. Caroline said they were reflections or echoes, like thinking a scrap of something in the middle of forgetting it. We didn't like forgetting, even though forgetting was always part of learning, so no one was jealous of Caroline's dreams, or even asked about them. Caroline would sit up on her cot and blink, and then tilt her head like a bird when it listens or looks at you. Irene would see her and ask. Sometimes Irene would tell Robbert.

And all of the time there was the wind and there was the ocean. Usually you only notice their noise when everything else is still. That's what Irene explained, though I think I heard them all the time. I paid special attention to the ocean—because of what Robbert said about fish, and because I couldn't swim, and because it was everywhere. I wasn't scared, though. I was never scared.

After we got dressed, we would go to the kitchen to help Irene make breakfast and boil water for her tea. She made a pot of Chinese tea first thing and then drank it over the whole day out of a white cup without a handle. She'd finish the very last of the pot before she went to bed, and, then, the next day do the same thing all over again. Since we always did the same things all the time, it was nice to see her do it, too. But for breakfast we made all kinds of things, whatever she felt like. We would mainly help with opening cans. Another thing she did in the morning was whistle. None of us could whistle, but we could sing. Irene taught us songs that we sang together, or in rounds— she liked us to sing in rounds—and often we would all sit on the porch, once breakfast had been cooked, singing just for her.

O wouldn't it be lovely
To dream a dream with you.
O wouldn't it be lovely
To dream a dream for two.

O won't you make me happy.
We'd never need to part.
O you could make me happy.
I'd give you all my heart.

Just we two in the sunset,
Drifting off across the sea.

After breakfast we would cross the courtyard to the class-room, but on the way we would take what Irene called a "ten-minute walk." Robbert's building was actually right next door, but we always started our trip to school the same way. This meant we could go anywhere we wanted, pick up anything, think of anything, only we had to be at the classroom in ten minutes, and then we had to talk about what we'd done or where we'd been. Sometimes Irene walked with us, which made it strange when we were back in the classroom, because we'd have to describe what we'd done, even though she'd been with us the entire time. But we learned she was listening to *how* we said things, not *what*, and to what we didn't talk about as much as what we did. Which was how we realized that a difference between could and did was a thing all by itself, separate from either one alone, and that we were being taught about things that were invisible.

When we did a ten-minute walk, we would go to the same place all together—all to the woods, or all peering under the kitchen steps, or all to an anthill.

One day we finished our ten-minute walk and, like always, each took a seat on our own bench. Irene and Robbert told us to pay attention to little things as much as big—at how little things *made* big things—so that morning we stood in the grass, which came to our faces, and paid attention to the insects buzzing around the feathered tops of the stalks, and to the warmth of the sun, and how cool the grass still was around our feet, and that there were different insects down there, hopping. That was what Isobel said, because she went first. The rest of us said the same thing, except Eleanor, who saw a little brown bird fly past, looking for bugs.

Irene said that was very good, and next it was time to take a nap, so we all stretched out on our benches. We could take naps at any time, no matter when or where, and when Irene woke us Robbert was with her, wiping his hands with a towel. She said we were going on another walk, only this would be for thirty minutes. What was more, we would be walking by ourselves. Each one of us had to go to a different place.

We were always excited to do something new, but it turned out to be harder than we thought, because we kept having the same ideas. Irene clapped her hands, and we all went down the stairs into the red dirt yard. I took a step toward the woods and saw that everyone else had, too. We stopped and, then after a moment, Caroline kept going to the woods. The other three of us were still stopped, but then we all stepped toward the cliffs. We stopped again, and Isobel went on to the cliffs. Eleanor and I both stepped to the beach. We stopped and then Eleanor walked to the beach, and I went the other way alone, the last way—toward the dock. I took three steps, then turned around. The other three had all stopped, too. We stood looking at each other. Irene called out that we were going to run out of time. So I got going to the dock.

The path to the dock is the only real path—made of crushed red gravel—on the island, instead of the other paths made by wearing down grass or going through bushes. Robbert and Irene needed it to wheel supplies from the dock with their cart, because some of the boxes could be heavy. The supply boat came once a month, but we never saw it. We never knew when it was scheduled, and it always seemed to come when we were napping. We slept a lot, but that was because we worked a lot. We worked very hard. Irene told us that all the time.

We didn't visit the dock very often. For one, we had to be very careful about the water, and for two there just wasn't any reason. The path cut through tall grass and then shorter grass and scrub, and then finally wound down to the shore. The dock stuck out on pilings from a big spur of black rock—there wasn't any beach—because that was where the water was deep enough for the supply boat. The dock planks had been soaked in creosote and tar but were now bleached by the sun. Walking onto the dock was a little like walking alone into the middle of the ocean, especially when I looked back and saw the island behind me.

The dock had metal cleats for the boat to tie up but no railing, so I was careful to walk in the exact center and stop before reaching the far end, which was the rule to keep everyone safe if they happened to fall down. It took twelve minutes to walk from the buildings to the dock, so I knew that with the return time I had six minutes to stand and look, at the big things and at the little. First, I crouched and studied the wooden planks. I peeled away a splinter and the wood underneath was a different color. I found two boards that had warped enough to open a crack between them, and through it I saw the water. Or I could see shadows, but I knew the shadows *were* the water—which made me think of the difference between water in the sunlight and water in the dark, and whether, since sunlight went *through* the water, they were even the same thing at all, and which had come first. Was dark water somehow more natural? Or was the dark ocean incomplete and the sunny ocean the finished version, like a sandwich with the final layer of mustard? Irene liked mustard on her sandwiches except for peanut butter, but she only ate peanut butter when there wasn't anything else, which is one way we knew the supply boat would be coming: sandwiches without mustard.

Before I left I looked up and saw two seagulls, so close that I could imagine how soft their feathers would be to touch. I watched until they disappeared around the other side of the island. I knew it would actually take me longer to go uphill than to go down, but still I stayed on the dock, surrounded by the idea of being alone. Another invisible.

When I did get back, the others were waiting on the porch. I waved as soon as I saw them, and they waved back. Irene sent us all inside, but before I reached the door Robbert touched my shoulder. The other three turned, watching through the doorway. Robbert asked if I knew that it had been thirty-five minutes, not thirty. I said I was sorry—I was looking at the water and there had been two birds. He told me to stop talking. Then he asked again, if I knew it had been thirty-five minutes instead of thirty. I told him that yes, I did know, but that I was in the middle of looking at things and thought that the looking was more important than the getting back. Robbert stopped me again. Then he asked me why I thought that—why did I possibly think that was true?

I didn't know. I'd just done it. I said I was sorry again. He sent me in the classroom with the others. Then he saw the others were watching and got sharp and told us to *all sit down right now*. We did, and stayed there while Irene and Robbert whispered on the porch. Then they came in and Irene asked what we'd seen on our walks.

I went first and told everything: the gravel, the dock, the splinter, the gap in the boards, the water, the sunlight, the sky, the birds—it took a while. When I finished, Irene said I'd done very well. The others just looked at me. Robbert reminded everyone about how dangerous the water was, and that going to the dock, just like going to the beach, shouldn't be a habit *for anyone*. Then he looked at me again, like he had on the porch, not quite with a smile—because it wasn't a smile—but with something.

Then Isobel told about her trip to the cliffs, and everything began to change, like the air in a room getting colder when a door is opened, because I realized that I was looking at Isobel like the others had looked at me. This is part of what she said:

"—one of the black crabs, but it was red on the bottom, bright red like sunburn or like hot sauce, and it was on its back and torn open, with four legs missing and the insides mostly gone, probably from birds except it was also wet, in a way that the cliff rocks *weren't* wet, like it had been wet since the tide had gone down. So I asked myself how a dead crab got wet on a rock that was dry, and I wondered if one of the birds had dropped it or if the crab had been wet and crawled out and *then* been attacked by a bird, or maybe if—"

And this is part of what Caroline said:

"—so I kicked it—because it was on the ground, like a ball, and it was old and dried out, so I knew it wouldn't be too heavy, so I *could* kick it—and it bounced off the trunk of the palm tree and rolled into the grass. I kicked it again, only this time farther into the grass, and it made a hole in the grass like a path, so I followed, and then kicked it again, in another direction, and it made another path, and I kept on kicking and walking, just where the coconut had rolled, so it wasn't me making the path but the coconut, and when I looked back the whole patch of grass looked like the tunnels in an anthill—"

And this is part of what Eleanor said:

"—counting waves, because the waves keep coming, even

though each one is different—where it breaks, how high, how fast, how much it's shaped like the waves before, or the waves after, or how far it comes in or comes out—today the tide was going out—and I looked at how the sand on the beach dried as the tide went away and thought about how long it would take to dry until I could walk on it—"

But I was outside of everything they said, like I listened to their stories through a window. I could imagine everything they said—I understood the words, but the understanding happened in me by myself, not in me with them. We'd done things separately before—Caroline had dreams, or one of us would visit Robbert while the others napped—yet this was different, because we all seemed to enjoy our time alone, but then felt strange when the others talked about *their* times alone, which didn't make sense.

I also knew that even though Robbert had specifically told me not to, I was going to go back to the dock the very first chance I could.

I couldn't even say why. There were birds all over. There was water all over. Was it the dock itself—that there could be a boat? But I hadn't seen any boat and hadn't thought about one either. Boats were only a bit less dangerous than planes, and they were the last thing I needed to be playing with—just like I didn't need to be too near the water.

So I asked.

"Why did we go to different places on our walk?"

Irene and Robbert paused, like they hadn't expected the question.

"So you'd learn about paying attention," said Irene.

Then it was time for dinner—the day had gone very quickly because of the long nap—and Irene led us from the classroom back to the kitchen. I was last going down the steps. Robbert was behind me and put his hand on my shoulder again, and I stopped. This time the others didn't notice and kept going. When they were inside the other building, Robbert let go.

"That was a curious question, Veronika."

I told him I was sorry, but he stopped me. He knelt to look into my eyes, like he wanted to see something on the other side of them.

"It was a good question. Why did you ask it?"

"Because we're paying attention to things we can't see."

He stood up and patted me on the head, and told me to go help Irene. He walked back into the classroom. I thought about following him, but I didn't.

Irene had the others helping make rice and opening cans of meat, so no one even noticed when I came in. When she saw me, Irene shoved a plastic bottle of mineral water to me, and I unscrewed the cap and then helped get out the plates and napkins and spoons and chopsticks. Robbert came in just before everything was ready and sat down, rubbing his eyes. He rubbed his eyes whenever he took off his glasses. Everyone helped carry things to the table.

After dinner Robbert went back to the classroom, and we sat with Irene on the porch, listening to the ocean and to the parrots, who were pretty loud. She asked us to sing. Eleanor asked what she would like to hear, and Irene told us to choose—she wanted to hear what we wanted to sing.

No one could decide. Irene touched my arm.

"Veronika, you asked a good question in school today, why don't you choose what to sing?"

She smiled. I started to sing, and the other three sang with me, happy to have it settled.

> *The honeybee flies in a line*
> *That zigs from side to side.*
> *To make its honey nectar wine*
> *It journeys far and wide.*
>
> *No matter where it finds itself*
> *A bee can find its home.*

We knew many more verses, all about bees—finding flowers,

drinking coconut milk, building hives, tending the queen—but all of them have the same chorus about bees finding their way home, no matter where they've gone. We kept singing until Irene said that was enough, and we watched the sunset until it was dark. Irene poured her last cup of tea and told us to get ready for sleep. We helped one another untie our smocks and fold them. We climbed onto our cots and waited for Irene to turn out the lights.

After five minutes she still hadn't come. Caroline turned to me and whispered. "What did Robbert say?"

"He wanted to know why I asked why we went on different walks."

"What did you say?"

"I said I was sorry."

"But you're not sorry," Eleanor whispered, from my other side. "Because I'm not sorry, either."

I nodded. I don't think I was ever sorry, really.

"What did *he* say?" whispered Caroline.

"He said it was a good question."

Everyone thought about that. Isobel whispered, from the other side of Caroline. "It is a good question." We all nodded and thought the same thing she said next. "That means they don't know what we're going to learn, either."

We heard Irene and stopped whispering. She came in, turned

out the light, and bent over each of our cots in turn. First Isobel, then Caroline, then Eleanor, then me, leaning close to my face and whispering, "Go to sleep, Veronika."

Then she pushed the spot behind my ear, with a click, like always, and I did.

2.

After that we always started mornings with thirty-minute walks, with each of us going a different direction. At first we just described what we'd seen, but since we had become so good at looking, this began to take up the whole morning. After a week, Robbert and Irene asked us to do things differently, because whenever we got good at something they would decide to change. They had us ask one another questions about comparing smells, or light, or sounds, or times—so we had to think about places we'd been to before as well as the place we'd just been now, and think about both in a way we hadn't either time. The questions weren't hard, but they were surprising. Each day we took naps and then helped with dinner. On special nights we went for a second walk with Irene in the dark, and then had an extra-late class to talk about *that*. The island was different at night, so we looked forward to night walks more than anything.

One night we went out after there had been a storm. It almost never rained on the island. Robbert always said that was what he liked about it, even though he didn't like to go out in the sun, either. We sometimes did see storms—the rain spattering against the windows and tapping on the roof like tiny hammers—but we never went out if it even looked like it might rain. Robbert always checked the weather very carefully on his notebook. For us the island meant sunshine and bright skies.

That night Irene took us to the beach, because all sorts of things could wash ashore in a storm, when the waves went higher than normal. We walked in a line, Irene leading the way with a flashlight. She would laugh and say her eyes "weren't as sharp as you kids"—but for us the beam became another thing to look at, bobbing in time with Irene's gait.

The beach path was sandy and soft, which meant we all took careful steps. Then the grass fell away and we stood between the dunes, looking out. The wave crests gleamed in the dark, tumbling onto the sand in lines of boiling foam. Different parts of the water moved at different speeds, and the waves were different heights and each one reached farther or stopped lower than the others. There were so many changes to see that all four of us stood motionless except for our flicking eyes and the wind whipping our hair.

Irene broke the spell, turning our attention to the sand, pointing out how high the storm had lifted the line of kelp and debris.
She told us the tide was going out, so the sand would be dry at
the top of the beach. Her feet dented its even surface, and she
flicked the light for us to follow. We did, walking slow because
sand is tricky. When we caught up, Irene aimed the flashlight at
a pile of kelp. She pulled it aside and underneath lay a tennis
shoe, the rubber bleached white and peeling. Irene poked at it
and said we could keep looking by ourselves, as long as we
stayed well away from the water.

We didn't move. Irene sighed, and then told Isobel to stay
with her and the three of us to go the other way, and to separate. She took Isobel by the arm and turned her to the debris.
The three of us began to walk without knowing what we were
looking for—what was worth studying and what wasn't. After
a minute, Caroline stopped and said she'd look around there.
She crouched and began to poke at the kelp with one hand,
like Irene. Eleanor and I kept walking until we'd gone the
same distance as between Irene and Caroline, and then Eleanor said she'd stop, too. I kept walking by myself until the
distance to Eleanor was the same as the distance from her to
Caroline, and from Caroline to Irene. When I looked back, I
saw that the beach curved more than I'd noticed. I couldn't
see Irene or Isobel at all. I couldn't even see Caroline. I looked

at Eleanor. She was crouched, but looking at me. I waved.

I turned around, careful not to look at the water, because if I looked too closely it would be hard to look away. Robbert called this pattern fixation. He laughed like it was a good thing, but always made an entry on his notebook, too. So I aimed my eyes at the sand, at what the storm had washed ashore: kelp, driftwood, plastic bottles, colored nylon rope, netting, lumps of Styrofoam—the usual things, but more of them than normal. I kicked at the bigger kelp lumps to see what was underneath—mostly more kelp. When I looked back, I couldn't see Eleanor.

Since I knew she wasn't far away, I kept going, eyes sharp for whatever Irene wanted to find. I was kicking so much that I almost didn't notice the prints of someone else kicking before me. I stopped. We'd all been inside, and the tide and the rain had made the sand flat, so any kicking would have had to have happened since then. This meant the prints had been made by Robbert, except he'd been in his room. Hadn't he? The line of kicked sand began down by the water, and the lowest ones had been half eroded by the waves. Because Robbert hated the water, he wouldn't have gone near it, so the kicks weren't his. The marks climbed all the way up the beach, into the grass. I looked behind me, but no one was there. I called to Eleanor but the wind snatched away the sound.

The grass was thick, but I pushed forward, the air whizzing

with insects as my steps stirred them from where they'd sat. I became so interested in how the insects flew that I almost tripped when my foot kicked something soft. Before me lay a shape that didn't make sense—all angles and bumps—swallowed by the grass like driftwood half buried in sand. I stared down, the spinning insects like thoughts that wouldn't settle to sense. Then all of a sudden, like with a puzzle, one shape became a leg, another an elbow, and it was a girl.

In the grass at my feet was a girl. She sprawled facedown, all wet, clothes tangled from the sea, hair flat across her face like a black mask.

I said, "Hello."

She didn't move.

I said, "Hello" again. Finally I bent to touch the exposed skin of her arm. It was soft and colder than Irene had ever been.

I hurried back as fast as I could without falling. When I saw Eleanor I began to wave. She waved back, but then stopped when she heard me yelling.

"I found her!"

I don't know why I expected Eleanor to know what I meant, but I yelled it anyway. Eleanor began waving in the other direction, to Caroline, and when I caught up to Eleanor we hurried together. I told her I found a girl washed up from the storm. When we reached Caroline, Irene and Isobel were coming from the other direction. I was in the middle of telling Caroline when they caught up. Irene told me to start over, slow and clear, telling *exactly* what I thought I found.

But I knew it was important, like the kitchen when a pot boils over, when instead of describing putting water in the pot and turning on the heat and putting in the noodles and then at last the boiling, that what you had to shout instead was just "the pot!"

"It's a girl," I told her. "I think she's dead."

Irene told the others to tell Robbert, and then she and I hurried down the beach. Her flashlight stabbed back and forth over our footprints, first three of us, then two of us and then just me. We got to the kicking marks and I pointed up to the grass. I didn't know I'd gone so far. I started to apologize, but Irene told me to stay where I was. She climbed into the grass and knelt down. I couldn't see her.

I could only hear the wind and the waves, the two sounds threaded together. Irene emerged with the girl in her arms. The hair still covered her face, and her limbs hung limp. I asked if she was dead.

"Not yet, Veronika. Quickly now." Irene brushed past, faster than me even, carrying the girl, because my feet were so slow in the sand. When I reached the classroom porch the other three were lined up, watching through the screen. I took my place without saying a word.

They'd put the girl on the big table, Robbert on one side, and Irene on the other. All we could see was Irene's back, and then beyond her the girl's bare legs. The light was sharp and narrow, but we could tell the girl's skin was brown, darker than any of us. The bottoms of her feet were crusted with sand and the skin was lighter, which made me think of the bleached tennis shoe. Robbert and Irene worked mostly around the girl's head, but after a while Irene leaned over her feet and rubbed the feet with a cloth daubed with alcohol. Once she washed off the sand, we could see the scuffed skin was actually bright red.

They worked for two hours, and we watched the entire time. Mostly Irene's and Robbert's bodies blocked our sight, but sometimes when they reached for a tool or medicine we would get a wondrous flash of this girl's different skin, whether smooth brown or torn raw. Finally Irene noticed us through the screen. She whispered to Robbert and came onto the porch, all of us backing up so she could open the door. Before we could say anything she whispered, "Let's go to your bedroom." She led us down the stairs and across the yard. The moon had come out, and the stars were bright. We followed her in.

Irene pointed to our cots and wouldn't say anything until we were ready for bed. Usually we had to untie our own smocks and fold them and make sure about the folding, but tonight, her fingers much faster than ours, she had the other smocks untied before the three of us could untie Eleanor's. Irene gathered them up as we lay down on our cots. She finished her folding and looked at us. We all looked back. Irene smiled, and spoke very carefully.

"The girl Veronika found in the grass is alive, and should be alive tomorrow. If she is, then she should be fine. She is probably from a ship, but whether she fell overboard, or whether it was wrecked in yesterday's storm, we don't know."

"I don't like accidents," said Isobel. We were all thinking of the accident that had killed our parents. We didn't know much more about what an accident actually was, only that they took people away and left others behind, just like this girl in the grass.

Caroline asked about the girl's skin being a different color, and Eleanor asked about her different hair, and I was about to ask about her parents when Irene held up her hand.

"She swallowed a lot of water, and she's been banged up by the rocks. We'll know more tomorrow."

She stood. This was her signal to turn off the light and put us to bed, but Isobel spoke again, in a whisper. "Do you know her name?"

"No. We don't know anything."

"Do you know how old she is?"

"We don't."

"Old as us?"

"We don't know, Isobel."

"Why does she look so different?" asked Caroline.

"Everyone looks different. I look different from you, and we all look different from Robbert. There's nothing strange about it." Irene turned off the light.

"What was under her skin?" I asked.

Irene looked at me. I almost thought she was angry, but then realized she didn't know how to answer my question, or couldn't decide.

"You've seen me cut my finger in the kitchen, Veronika."

"But this was different. It was more. And more different than a look."

Irene frowned. "What is a look?"

"A thing you see. On a surface. This was something else, wasn't it? Something more."

Irene watched me for a moment. "We'll talk about it tomorrow."

When we woke the day was hot and the clock said two in the afternoon—at least five hours past our normal time, maybe because we'd stayed up late the night before. Irene's hair was pulled back, and her face looked puffed and tired. I put on my smock and traded ties with Caroline. Irene waited on the steps, sitting with her teacup in both hands. When we were all behind her, she stood, but instead of leading us to the classroom, she went the other way, deeper into the island.

"Robbert is asleep. He was awake all night. The girl is asleep, too. We think she's going to live, though it's too soon to tell how badly she's been hurt. All that means is we're not going to have school in the classroom. We're going on a walk, and then the five of us will talk about what we saw, just like a normal day. I'm going to wait here, and each of you will go a different direction. Come back in forty-five minutes."

She sat on a palm log and took another swallow from her mug. Forty-five minutes was a very, very long time.

"Go," said Irene, with just a flick of impatience.

Without thinking why, I went toward the beach. Eleanor wanted to walk that way, too, but I didn't stop, and after a few steps she shifted to the woods. Normally I would have stopped, or at least thought about stopping, but this time I didn't.

The tide was halfway up the beach, but there was still dry sand where I could walk. I went the same way I had the night before, now under an open blue sky, looking for details. I had come back to finish what I'd started by finding her—though what there was left to finish, I couldn't imagine. Perhaps it was because I couldn't imagine that I was determined to look.

Half-buried shells and coral lay scattered by the waves, like the remains of writing mostly wiped away. The sand above the waterline still held a jumble of footprints, mine and Irene's—her prints pushing deeper when she'd been carrying the girl. I looked for the print of another foot altogether, the girl's bare, injured foot, but she must have been crawling. That's why her tracks were odd, which was why I even noticed them.

I climbed into the grass. In the sunlight where she'd lain was a tiny place, just a flattened circle. In a day or two, the grass would spring back and nothing would be left to tell what had happened. Then I saw, half hidden in the grass, a green nylon bag. It was dusted in sand, which fell off like powder when I picked it up. It was the size of a big book, with a zipper and a strap. I unzipped one side and peeked in. Then I sat down in the grass and unzipped it all the way.

The bag was stuffed full: a wadded cotton shirt, short nylon pants, a pair of plastic flip-flop shoes, a tube of sunscreen, a deck of playing cards, a string of green beads, and a small hard plastic square with buttons and a little dark screen. Last was a zipped-up rubber pouch with seven photographs. The water hadn't gotten in, and they weren't stuck together. I laid the pictures on the grass, as if seeing all seven would tell me more than looking one by one.

The first picture was taken from a boat, looking at a dock much bigger than ours and covered with boxes and crates. Leaning against the crates were two men, taller than Robbert, with bare feet and dark skin, smiling at the camera. It felt like meeting new people, because the men were smiling right at me, even though I knew they were actually smiling at someone else, at whoever was holding the camera, and however long ago that was.

I wondered if feeling these two things at once was like Caroline's dreams.

The second picture was also from the boat, but aimed over a metal rail across the water and beyond, at a jagged green line on the horizon, an island. The sky was gray, and the top of the island crowned with fog. I noticed the wedge of foam on the water and realized the boat had been *moving*.

The third picture showed a big blue and yellow parrot in a cage.

The fourth picture was *from* an island because it showed a beach, with palm leaves hanging into view. But most of the picture was of the ocean, facing west, because of the sun setting bright orange.

The fifth picture was a man holding a fish. He was knee deep in the ocean, and smiling. His skin was dark, and he had a round stomach that poked from under his T-shirt. The fish had a silver belly and green fins.

The sixth picture must have been inside the boat: a little room, with bunk beds and a foldout table, lots of shelves, and a hanging lamp. The man holding the fish in the fifth picture sat at the table, still smiling, with a plate of food.

The last picture was the girl herself, sitting on the wooden deck of a boat. She wore a green shirt without sleeves and showing her finger, which had a bright pink bandage wrapped around the tip. Her hair was tied back. Her eyes were brown. Her teeth were small and white. Her skin was dark, with darker freckles in a stripe below each eye and across her nose. It was a face unlike any I had seen.

The bandage made me think of her insides. We'd seen Robbert cut himself from shaving, and Irene cut herself on a can, so we knew about blood, but what had happened to the girl in the ocean was a door opening wider—not that we hadn't been told, but just that we hadn't been told everything.

I looked at the pictures again and again, laying them in different arrangements, and began a list of questions so I had something to say to the others, to Robbert and Irene, or to the girl when she woke up and needed to know who'd found her things. That made me think about what she might say about her boat, or about being in the water, or what she'd say if she went on one of our walks. What would her voice even sound like? Like Irene, or like one of us?

I had too many thoughts and no idea how to put them in order. What was the name of the parrot? Who was the man with the fish? Who were the men on the dock? Who cooked the food on the plate? What was the name of the boat? Which bunk belonged to the girl? Did she eat the fish? What was the name of the island? What was inside the crates and boxes? What had she done to her finger? What was it like on a moving boat? Was the man on the boat her father? What had he said to make her smile?

A shadow fell over the pictures. I looked up to see Irene, blocking the sun. I said hello and began to show her the pictures and the bag. She stopped me and asked if I knew what time it was. I said it was more than forty-five minutes. She asked me how *much* more, and I answered that it had been almost ninety minutes. She said she'd been watching me from the beach, just to see if I'd notice, but I hadn't. I told her that part of me had noticed, but that the other parts were concentrating very hard.

"You were supposed to come back forty-five minutes ago. You knew that, didn't you?"

"Yes, Irene."

"Then why are you still here?"

I didn't know. I'd just done it. I'd found things I'd never found before, but how did I choose they were more important? How did I choose without even noticing the choice?

I began again to tell her about the pictures and the bag and the beads. She told me to stop talking. She watched me for a moment, then gathered all the different things back in the bag. She looked through the photos once, slowly, and put them back in the rubber bag, zipped it, and then put that in the green bag, too. Then she handed the bag to me and told me I could carry it back. Irene walked slowly on the uneven sand, staying with me.

The others stood on the kitchen porch. When I saw them I waved. They waved back. When we got a little closer I waved again. They waved, too. I looked over to Robbert's building. The door was shut.

Irene led us into the kitchen and, without a word, started making dinner. We watched her open a can of soup and pour it into a pan and put it on the stove. We listened for the clicks before the burner caught, and then the rush of the flame. Irene called over her shoulder.

"Aren't you going to show the others, Veronika?"

As soon as she spoke, I realized I'd been waiting, but not for what. Irene's permission? Or did I want to keep thinking about the girl's things for myself? Why?

I put the bag on the table and unzipped it, placing each item on the table.

"It was in the grass," I said. "Covered in sand."

The others nodded, staring. Isobel picked up the flip-flops, and then handed them to Caroline, who handed them to Eleanor, who put them delicately back in their original spot. They went through every object, passing them along, not saying a word, just like I hadn't said a word. When Eleanor set down the string of green beads, they looked up at me again. I unzipped the bag of photographs and laid them on the table, feeling all my own thoughts compound inside the others' minds with each new image.

Before I could talk, Irene placed a hand on my shoulder. She wanted me to wait. She nodded at the others, and I understood I was supposed to watch—that this was another new thing, right in front of me. Once again we were becoming different from one another, or I was becoming different from them.

Or I was *already* different, just like Caroline, except in my own way?

All three kept flicking their eyes from picture to picture, like birds hovering over something they hadn't decided how to eat. They were forming questions and putting things together, but again I knew something more. I knew how hurt she had been and how far she had crawled. It was a difference I could only compare to spending ninety minutes on the beach instead of forty-five. I still didn't know how that could happen, I just knew that it had.

The others were still staring at the pictures when we heard Robbert on the porch. We all turned to see him step inside, looking at Irene.

"She's awake," he said.

3.

Irene asked Robbert if he wanted to eat the rest of her soup. He glanced at us—we were all looking at him—and took her place at the table. We heard Irene's feet go down the stairs and her steps on the path and then, because we were listening, the hinges of Robbert's screen door wheeze open and clack shut. Robbert poked his chin at what I'd found, spread out on the table.

"What's this?"

It took a long time to tell, though now the others could tell it, too, and so they helped. Robbert had questions, just like Irene, but his questions were different, like between a sandwich with mustard and without, or a wet stone and a dry one, or the sounds of night compared to day. Partly this was because Irene had seen all the girl's things for herself, out in the grass. But even so,

Robbert's questions weren't about his own thinking—though we could all see that he *was* thinking—but about the words we used to describe each object, and most especially the pictures.

When he finished his soup he set the bowl down with enough of a noise that Caroline, who was comparing the boxes in the picture of the dock to the boxes from our supply boat, stopped talking. Robbert wiped his lips on the back of one hand and took off his glasses. He blew on them, held them to the light, and frowned. Whenever he did this, we stared at his face, as if his eyes were naked. I had never seen Robbert naked, or Irene, but I knew what we looked like without our smocks, and whenever I saw Robbert's unprotected eyes it felt like I was looking at the same uncovering—but even more so, like a crab flipped on its back, showing the seams in the shell where the birds stick their beaks in.

He put his glasses back and coughed. "The first picture." He picked it up, so we all faced him in order to see. "Describe it in one word. No repeats. Start with Isobel."

The first picture showed the two men on the dock piled with boxes.

"Dock," said Isobel.

"Supplies," said Caroline.

"Friends," said Eleanor.

I was last, thinking of what hadn't been said. "Girl."

Robbert sniffed high up in his nose and coughed again. "Good. Each of you chose a word for just part of the picture, one that hadn't been named. Except for Veronika, who described the picture being taken."

"Is that allowed to be part of the picture?" asked Eleanor.

"What do *you* think?"

Unlike Irene, Robbert's questions almost always had a wrong answer. Instead of saying anything, we had learned to wait a moment and then nod.

"All right," said Robbert. "Let's try again, with the next picture. . . ."

The second photograph showed the line of green across the water, taken from a moving boat.

"Island," said Isobel.

"Ocean," said Caroline.

"Wind," said Eleanor.

"Boat," I said.

"Good," said Robbert. "Eleanor, why wind?"

"Because of the moving boat," said Eleanor. "Because of how cold it looks and since you said only one word."

Robbert nodded. He picked up the hard plastic square with the dead screen. He turned it over and, then with both hands, snapped open the back of the square. He blew on the thin piece that had come free and tipped the rest of the square, smiling at the little stream of water that dribbled into his bowl. He set both pieces down.

"We'll let it dry. All right. Next picture." This was the big parrot in a cage.

"Parrot," said Isobel.

"Cage," said Caroline.

"Feathers," said Eleanor.

"Prison," I said.

"Good. Better. Veronika, if you'd been first, would you have said parrot?"

I nodded.

"Is that the best word? Is it better than 'prison'?"

"It's more of the picture."

"That's not what I asked. Is it *better*? Which would you say first—not then, but *now*, now that you know both of them?"

"I would still say 'cage,'" said Caroline.

"Good. Why?"

"Because there's a cage."

"No. That's wrong."

"But there is a cage," protested Caroline.

"And that's the wrong reason. Eleanor. Why would cage be right?"

"Because the cage is between the camera and the parrot—you see it first."

"Wrong."

"But you do."

"And that isn't the right reason, either. Isobel?"

"I think cage is wrong because I already said the best word which is parrot."

Robbert smiled. "Almost. Almost, but just *exactly* wrong. Veronika. If you were alone and had to say one word and the word you said was cage—why would that be right?"

He looked at me through his glasses, impatient for the answer but also impatient at being with us at all, to be spending time asking questions whose answers he already knew when there was so much other work, so many answers he didn't know waiting in his building. This was why, while Robbert was never as nice and we much preferred Irene's company, we always tried harder to please him.

"Because the parrot is the biggest thing in the picture," I said.

"Explain."

"Because it's the one word you *don't* have to say. So if you say cage it's like you're already saying parrot at the same time."

Robbert looked at each one of us in turn. "That is correct. Do you understand? Who understands? Caroline."

"We have to pretend that all four of us are answering the question even though it's only one of us. We have to sort through."

"Exactly."

"Why?"

"What?"

"Why?" repeated Isobel. "Why do we have to pretend there's only one of us."

"Because that might be the case," said Robbert. "Just like on a thirty-minute walk. Just like when Veronika found our guest. There may only be time to do one thing. You need to know what that one thing is, and you do it by thinking."

We all nodded, but no one asked what they wanted to ask, which was to ask Isobel's question again, because no one felt Robbert had answered it—not what she had *really* asked. But no one thought, if it was asked again, that Robbert would get anything but snappy.

"What is Irene doing?" Caroline had her head cocked, like when she woke up from her dreams.

"I'm sure she'll tell you when she's done." Robbert looked at his watch, then yawned. "Maybe it's time for a nap."

We didn't want to take a nap and as it turned out we didn't have to. Instead, Robbert rubbed his eyes and announced we would go for a walk. He shooed us in front of him and stumped down the stairs, the dangling tips of his shoelaces tapping the wood. We stood in the yard, waiting for Robbert to tell us where to go, but he yawned again and stood staring at the classroom. We stared, too.

"What are all you looking at?" he called. "Let's go. This is a thirty-minute walk. Thirty minutes exactly. Alone and in different directions than you've gone before. Everyone should be thinking about parrots and cages. Stay away from the water. *Go*."

We all looked at one another, taking half steps and changing directions again and again until we were sorted. Eleanor went to the cliff, Caroline to the beach, and Isobel toward the dock. I ended up walking between the buildings toward the woods. Since both the beach and the cliff could show new things washed up from the storm, and Isobel would be at the dock, I wondered if any of the others would decide to forget about time, too?

I kept to the path until I reached the palms. The wind rustled the leaves and the treetops waved against the sky. I went to where the trees stood tight together, the ground between piled with branches and old husks. Birds lived in the tops of the palms, and other things lived in the dead branches and husks, rats and lizards and all kinds of bugs. If it was quiet you could hear them move.

I looked at the pile, trying to think of parrots and cages. There were parrots in the trees—probably right then, above me—but that wasn't what Robbert meant. If I was looking at palm trees, I should be thinking something *else*. But I couldn't think of anything. I turned around. On the far side of the meadow stood Robbert's building.

Halfway back I left the path and entered the grass, bending

until it rose above my head. Crickets launched themselves around me. At the edge of the grass, I squatted lower. Robbert's building stood on cinder-block stilts. I crept behind a stilt so no one on the other side, if they looked underneath, could see me. Most of Robbert's back windows weren't windows anymore at all, but mesh-covered exhaust vents, for machines. The only window left was right where I stood. I looked in.

This was the back room, all cabinets and boxes, but the door was ajar, and beyond it lay the foot of Robbert's bed. The white sheet had been kicked away—which I knew because I could see the foot that had kicked it, now strapped with white bandages. I heard different machines, and I wondered if any of them were helping the girl.

Irene came through the door and I ducked down. I heard her flipping switches and peeked up. She held a dark page up to the light, and the page became a picture of a gray arm with white bones. The girl's arm, though it wasn't really gray. We'd seen bird's bones, and fish, even rats. But those bodies had feathers or scales or fur, a covering. Were the bones inside her really white? Were there the same dark pages of me? Irene snapped off the lamp and walked out. I retreated to the grass. It was almost time.

I reached the yard almost exactly when Eleanor and Isobel did. Robbert rose from where he'd been sitting on the kitchen steps, swatting dust off the seat of his pants. When he saw Caroline wasn't there, he looked off toward the beach, then climbed onto the porch and looked again.

"Stay here." Robbert jumped off the steps and broke into a jog. *"Stay!"* he called over his shoulder, and disappeared.

We stood in the yard, thinking about where he'd gone.

"If something was wrong he would have called for Irene," said Eleanor. "But he didn't. That's because of Veronika not coming back before. Caroline might have decided something new was more important, too."

"Except Robbert is also afraid of the water," Isobel said. "He told me to stop at the end of the path, before I reached the dock."

"Did you see a boat?" asked Eleanor. "Maybe the two men in the picture have come looking for her."

Isobel shook her head. "I saw a storm petrel."

"Maybe the two men drowned," said Eleanor.

We turned at the wheeze of the classroom screen door. "Where is Caroline?" Irene called.

We pointed to the beach. Irene went to the edge of the porch and craned her head, but you couldn't see the beach path from there, so she came to us—none of us saying anything, since she wasn't saying anything—and went on her toes. Irene dropped to her flat feet and frowned.

"Go sit on the kitchen porch, all of you. Stay there."

The kitchen steps meant we still weren't using the classroom, where the girl was sleeping. We got halfway to it before we realized Irene was gone. We stopped to watch her disappear, as if Irene's leaving had become another problem we'd been set to solve.

"Caroline is the parrot," said Isobel. "And there's something else on the beach."

"Or the beach is the parrot," said Eleanor. "And something happened to Caroline."

We couldn't know which until Robbert or Irene came back and told us.

"Did you go to the cliffs?" I asked Eleanor.

She told us what she'd seen: different colors of Styrofoam, plastic bottles, plastic bags, and one shoe, all floating near the rocks. Isobel asked about the shoe, but Eleanor said it was too far away to tell the size. She asked me about the trees, and I described going to the window instead, and the picture of bones.

"Why did you go there?" asked Isobel, but then she answered her own question, both eyes blinking. "You decided the parrot was the girl."

When Robbert asked why I'd stayed at the dock instead of coming back on time, I'd known what I'd done, but not why. The why felt like a little hole somewhere inside, and now, even though I couldn't name the feeling, it was happening again. The three of us ought to have been sitting on the steps, but we were all standing in the yard. Then, like three birds keen on the same crab, we turned to look at Robbert's porch.

"They could some back," said Eleanor. "I'll see them sooner from the kitchen porch."

As if this decided everything, Isobel and I crossed the yard. At the top of Robbert's steps we looked to Eleanor, who stood on the kitchen porch, staring out. She shook her head—no one was coming.

Very carefully, quietly, we pressed our faces against the screen.

Right inside was the empty classroom. The room was dim, dotted with blinks and blips from different machines. The bed was against the wall, the shape upon it still. Isobel opened the door so slowly that the squeak turned to a long soft sigh.

Bottles and wadded towels cluttered the table by the bed. The girl's clothes were heaped on a countertop, and Robbert's desk had been cleared to make room for books, left open next to the keyboard and big screens. On top of the books lay a glossy stack of dark pages, more bone pictures.

We crept to the bed. The girl had rolled toward the wall, so we couldn't see her face. Her breathing was a faint, clogged whistle. Her hair was damp on the nape of her neck. One arm lay flung out, wrapped round with white stripes of tape and gauze.

"Zebra," whispered Isobel.

The girl's breath caught, as if she'd heard. We didn't move. The machines hummed quietly, hives of sleeping bees. We never woke up without Irene rousing us, and since this girl was so extra tired, we decided we were safe. But just then we heard Eleanor across the courtyard, high-pitched and shrill.

"They're coming back! They're coming back!"

The girl sat up at the noise. She looked right at us. We didn't move, and for a moment neither did she. Then her eyes got wide. Her mouth shot open and she screamed.

We got out of Robbert's building as fast as we could, banging open the screen and racing down the steps. I expected more screams behind us, but we only heard Eleanor.

"What happened? What happened?"

Before we could answer, she pointed past us to the beach, where Irene's and Robbert's heads bobbed above the curve of the path. Then Caroline's head was visible, too, walking hand in hand with Irene. Robbert had something heavy in his arms.

I looked back to Robbert's door, wondering if the girl had climbed out of the bed, if she was there looking out at us. "What happened?" whispered Eleanor, again.

"She woke up," I said.

"Do you think they heard?" asked Isobel.

"It was loud," said Eleanor.

Irene and Caroline waved and we all waved back. By now I could see that Robbert carried a big bundle of white cloth. He got to the middle of the yard and set it down and began to unwrap it, tugging and kicking at the roll. I didn't see anything inside except sand.

Caroline came up the steps. Irene called for us to go inside and wait. Then she walked to the classroom. Robbert said something to her as she passed, but we couldn't hear it.

"What are you looking at?" asked Caroline, who had opened the door and didn't know why no one else was coming.

"The girl," said Isobel.

"What about her?"

"We went inside."

"Did they tell you not to?"

"Irene said stay on the porch," said Eleanor.

Irene disappeared into the classroom. Robbert spread the last corner of cloth to dry. It covered half the yard. He saw us watching him.

"Didn't Irene send you inside?"

We all went for the door, bunching up so no one could get through.

"Wait!"

We looked back at Robbert. He wiped his hands on his pants.

"Did Irene send you inside or not?"

"Yes, Robbert." We all answered at once.

"Then why aren't you?" His voice was tired, but serious. This time no one answered. "Go. Sit on your cots and wait."

Isobel and I sat looking at Caroline, wondering what had happened on the beach. She was looking at us because Eleanor looked at us, too, which told Caroline something had happened that Eleanor hadn't seen. Everyone wanted the others to talk, but we knew that when Irene got there she'd have us talk in just the way she wanted and we were supposed to wait. After not doing what she'd asked so many times, no one wanted to disappoint her. So no one said anything, except finally Isobel.

"What if she tells Irene?" A clump of her yellow hair was out of place, flipped up, from hurrying across the yard.

"What she?" asked Caroline.

Irene came up the steps and in. She went to her table and poured a cup of tea. She sipped, then smiled, as if she'd just realized that she hadn't been smiling and hoped we hadn't noticed. Then she asked Caroline to tell everyone what she'd found.

As Caroline talked, Irene watched the rest of us. I didn't know if this was because she already knew the story and didn't care, or something else, so I did my best to listen.

Caroline hadn't come back from the beach because she'd found too many new things washed up from the storm. The largest thing, now spread across the yard, was a sail, which Caroline knew could be useful in all kinds of ways and so she'd tried to drag it back. It had been heavier than she'd expected and her feet had become half buried in the sand from pulling. She'd been able to get free of the sand, but by that time she was late. When Robbert had found her she explained and pointed to all the other things still on the beach. Then Irene arrived, and she and Caroline looked at the beach while Robbert pulled the sail free of the sand and folded it up. What they'd found wasn't so interesting after all—plastic bottles, plastic bags, coconuts, and more Styrofoam.

Then Irene asked Eleanor about the cliff, Isobel about the dock, and me about the woods. I told her about looking at the circle of palm trees—which I had—but as if I'd done that for the entire time. Was it because I wasn't finished thinking about what I'd seen? Why did I care if those questions stayed mine?

"Did you hear anything?" she asked. "Any animals?"

I shook my head.

"Not at all?" she asked.

I shook my head again. "It was too windy in the leaves."

"Well. Another busy afternoon. I think it's time for naps."

When Irene woke me the other three were still sleeping on their cots. Irene was behind me, doing up the top tie of my smock. She patted my back, which was a signal to sit straight. She gently wiped my hair with a cloth and then walked around to pour another cup of tea.

"How do you feel, Veronika?"

"Very well," I said. "Did you have a nap, too?"

"No, I've been talking to the others."

I nodded. We preferred to be talked to all together.

"And I've been talking to our guest."

Irene waited. I was supposed to say something. "Will she die?"

"No. She should be fine."

"What's her name?"

Irene smiled. "I don't know, yet."

"Be sure to ask," I said. "We're very curious."

"I will." Irene went to pour more tea but the pot was almost empty. Usually one pot lasted to after dinner. "How would you feel, Veronika, if Caroline had found other things on the beach today, but hadn't told you about them?"

"Why not?"

"Because I asked her not to."

"Why would you do that?"

"Can you answer my question first? How would that make you feel?"

"It would depend on if it's true."

"It is."

"Then I don't understand."

"Are there things you haven't told me?"

I didn't know what to say, but finally got to "There are things you haven't asked."

"All right. What haven't I asked?"

My eyes were blinking. I was used to guessing why Irene asked questions—because we were learning how to learn—but I didn't know enough to guess about the girl. Would she go home? Would she join us in the schoolroom? Or, even though Irene told me no, was she going to die after all?

"About her," I finally said.

"Did you go with Isobel into Robbert's building?"

"Yes."

"Did the girl see you? Think carefully. It's very important."

"She did. She screamed out loud. But when we ran away she didn't do anything, so maybe she didn't."

Irene nodded, but I was blinking again and she waited for me to finish.

"Why would she scream?" I asked.

Irene took a moment to answer. "We don't know what happened to her, or the people she was with."

"The men on the dock?"

"Possibly. Or other people. Her family."

"Why would they teach her to scream?"

"Not everyone is taught as carefully as you, Veronika."

"Why not?"

"That's a good question, but it's for later. Now, if I ask you something, will you promise to do it?"

"Yes, Irene."

"I want you to stay away from Robbert's building—not even going on the porch."

"What about the classroom?"

"We'll use the kitchen. Until I say otherwise. This is very important. Do you promise?"

"Just me, or everyone?"

"Everyone."

"I promise."

"Good." Irene put down her empty cup and picked up a clipboard. She gave it a scowl, because she didn't want to put on her glasses, then set it back on the table. "Now, let's talk about why we make decisions."

Whenever they talked to us alone we tried to decide why. Irene asked me questions for an hour, about my visits to the dock and to the beach, and then about Isobel and me going in to see the girl, especially about whose idea it had been and how we had decided. She never asked more about that afternoon, so I didn't tell about looking in the window, because since all our talking was questions there wasn't room. Irene made sure we answered exactly, and she'd repeat a question until we got it right.

But maybe we'd spent too much time talking about the parrot to forget Robbert's lesson about looking, because I saw how all of Irene's questions pointed the same direction—how together they formed a cage and how behind them lay a thing that didn't need saying to be felt.

When I stretched out on my cot, I asked Irene where Robbert was sleeping if the girl was in his bed.

"In the attic of the classroom," she said. "It won't be for long."

"Why not?"

"Because it's only temporary. Now, while you're asleep I want you think of something."

I nodded. Irene often gave us ideas to think about before falling asleep and asked us about them in the morning. Caroline always had an idea. Sometimes the rest of us had things to say, and sometimes we didn't.

"I want you to think about all the ways we could use the sail-cloth Caroline found. Will you do that?"

I nodded, but still had my question. "Irene?"

"Yes, Veronika."

"What should we do if she comes to look at us?"

Irene smiled at me. It was a nice smile, and all the answer I got.

• • •

I don't know why I asked. Maybe at the chance we might get sick as well, that one of us could be tangled up on Robbert's bed. But the next morning, while we helped with breakfast, I saw Eleanor staring at a floor tile near the door. On purpose I dropped the spoon I was holding and bent to pick it up, so I could look at the tile more closely. At Eleanor's feet lay a fresh smear of dirt and grass, which might have come from Irene's sandal or Robbert's sneaker if it hadn't been topped by the dusty dots of small round toes.

4.

That morning our class was in the kitchen. Irene had us study temperature and the barometer and the satellite map on Robbert's notebook, so we could carry numbers in our heads to compare with how things would feel outside later on. After helping her make lunch—miso soup, from a waxed paper pouch instead of a can—the five of us took the red gravel path to the dock. We listened to the wind and the water, and peered at the seaweed and mussels and barnacles. We measured the speed of the wind and the position of the absent moon and the exact point the tide would turn. That these were questions we could answer—that the answers were numbers—made a change from the walks about deciding what to say, walks where we had too many answers and had to find, like guessing a bird from its shadow, a question that fit them.

Yet, especially since I'd found the girl, we had become more used to stories and guessing, like we'd turned a page in a book, so when this walk with Irene seemed like everything we'd almost stopped doing, we were confused. But doing numbers instead of stories was just another parrot in a cage: while part of me tracked the moon, another part saw it as one task I did instead of another and then, because this was our new habit, I asked myself why. So there were always two questions, or always one question more—since sometimes Irene's problems got complicated—than we'd been directly asked.

We didn't mention this out loud. That was a test, and to ask Irene was either to pass or to fail. The true test was knowing before you asked what the answer would be—and since we couldn't work it out, none of us said a word.

Caroline and I walked back on either side of Irene, holding her hands, since Isobel and Eleanor held her hands on the way down. Holding Irene's hand was different every time: her skin was soft, but also just a little loose, so exactly where it would wrinkle and where it would stretch was always special. Sometimes we squeezed too much and she would ask us to be more gentle, but usually she just held out her hands for us to take, and one of us would say "And no pinching!" Irene would always smile and reply, "That's right" to whoever had spoken.

The path back climbed a small hill before the rocks changed

to scrub and grass—just before you could see the kitchen roof. Irene released our hands and told us to wait, then kept walking for another thirty yards, until the top of her head disappeared. Then we saw Irene's hand in the air, like a moth flapping back and forth. She was waving to Robbert.

I looked at Caroline. "Irene said you found something else on the beach that you're not supposed to talk about."

Caroline only nodded, as if answering out loud would be against Irene's instructions.

Eleanor tugged on Caroline's smock. "What was it?"

"What was it?" echoed Isobel.

"I can't say," whispered Caroline. "I *can't.*"

"Why *not?*" asked Isobel.

"We have to guess," said Eleanor. "Was it alive?"

Caroline shook her head, but before we could ask more questions we saw Irene coming back.

Caroline and I took her hands again. Robbert waited on the kitchen steps, and even held the door open as we went inside. Across the yard, the classroom door was closed.

For two days we worked on numbers, preparing in the morning and then walking one day to the beach for waves and the next to the woods to study palms. Both days, on our way back, Irene left us at the spot on the trail just before we could see the buildings and went ahead to wave. It was only returning from the woods, when I saw where I'd stood behind Robbert's building, that I understood what she was doing. We knew we weren't supposed to see the girl, but the girl was being kept from us as well. We hadn't noticed that our singing on the steps had been skipped three nights in a row—we'd all just gone to bed early. Eleanor and I had told Isobel and Caroline about the footprint. We knew the girl had seen us twice—us by her bed, and her standing over ours. We would have mentioned the footprint if Irene or Robbert had asked, but for those days it was as if the girl didn't exist, and we were just too good at focusing to talk out of turn.

But that night, after the woods, we were helping Irene with dinner—folding napkins and setting out chopsticks and spoons—when Robbert came in. Irene said everything was almost ready, but Robbert just poked his chin up at Irene's room, then climbed the stairs ahead of her. Irene sighed and turned down the burner flame and wiped her hands and followed. Since there was no door, we could still hear, even though they spoke quietly.

"What's wrong?" she asked.

"We have to decide."

"We have another week, don't we? I thought we agreed . . ."

Their footsteps went farther from the stairs. We could only hear murmurs and the purr of burning gas.

Irene hadn't run out of mustard yet, but I wondered if another week meant the next supply boat. I didn't know what else could happen in a single week, unless another storm had been predicted.

From the darkened yard behind us came the faintest squeak, a metallic sliver of sound we all recognized as the screen door of the classroom. The murmurs kept going upstairs. They hadn't heard.

All four of us crept to our screen and looked out. The girl was outside. She slipped down the classroom steps into the yard, and then she stopped, hunkering down. She looked at our door, maybe even at our shapes, shadows with the light behind us. In a burst, like a rat from under a palm frond, she darted toward us, right under the kitchen porch and out of view. Robbert and Irene were still talking. The water had begun to boil.

"Watch the pan," I said. I opened the door.

"What if they come down?" whispered Eleanor.

But I didn't answer. I'd already seen the girl and she'd seen me—so what could be the harm? The others caught the screen so it closed without a sound. I went down the stairs, holding the rail like always. At the bottom I looked under the building. She was on her knees in the weeds, peeking past the middle stilt. We watched each other.

"Hello," I finally whispered. "Are you feeling better?"

The girl didn't answer.

"I found you on the beach," I said.

She kept crouching there.

"I'm Veronika."

"What *are* you?" Her voice was as different as the rest of her, close to a croak.

"I'm Veronika. This is our island. What's your name?"

It took her a little while to decide, but she finally did. "May."

"That's short," I said. "Our names are longer. Are you sure that's all of it?"

"What are you?" she asked again. I had no idea what to say.

"I'm Veronika. The other girls are Isobel and Eleanor and Caroline."

"Girls?"

"Why don't you come into the kitchen?"

"He told me not to."

"But you already did, didn't you?" She nodded. I nodded back to be friendly. "Don't worry. Now you're safe."

"Who are they?"

"Irene and Robbert. They take care of us. Why don't you come out?"

I'd been too long. When I looked up, Irene and Robbert stood in the doorway. I went back to my crouch and called to her.

"Everyone wants to meet you, May. And it's dinnertime. Aren't you hungry?"

• • •

Irene and Robbert left it to me. Eventually May came out and up the stairs. I waited and held out my hand for her to take, which she did, hesitating and looking at Irene and Robbert to see if it was okay. I knew not to squeeze (or pinch) and just let her fingers do the feeling. She looked different than she had in the beach grass or on the bed, much closer to how she looked in the photograph, even if she didn't smile. Most of the zebra bandages were gone from her arms, but her feet still had a few, so she wore the flip-flops from her bag. Her shirt had been in the bag, too, short-sleeved with colored flowers, so someone must have washed it. We climbed into the light and I saw her more clearly than ever. May's hair was as black as Eleanor's but thick and curled where Eleanor's just hung. Her skin was almost the color of Irene's peanut butter, but darker. Her face had a long patchy scab, like a paintbrush had been dragged down her cheekbone to her chin.

Irene opened the door. May let go of my hand, and at a nudge from Robbert I went to Isobel, Caroline, and Eleanor, all of us staring at May as nicely as possible.

"May has met Veronika already," said Robbert. "This is Isobel, Eleanor, and Caroline."

May just looked at us.

"Isobel has blond hair," said Robbert. "Caroline has brown hair like Irene, and Eleanor has black hair, just like you."

May didn't say anything about hair. Robbert touched her shoulder, gently.

"Everything is fine, May."

"What can you girls say to make May feel welcome?" asked Irene.

"Do you eat soup, May?" asked Isobel. "We made soup for dinner."

"Do *you* eat soup?" May's voice was still raspy.

"We *make* soup," replied Caroline. "And all kinds of things. Tonight there's noodles."

"Why don't we set another place?" said Irene. "Come to the table, May, take a seat."

Irene pulled a stool from the counter and set it between her chair and Robbert's. May sat down, hugging her arms even though it wasn't cold. We all fetched another table setting—spoon, chopsticks, plate, bowl, cup—and set them down in the proper order. Robbert poured water from the filter jug into her cup, and then shook a yellow pill from a plastic bottle.

"May needs to take this after she eats," he told us. "It will help her sleep, so she can heal more quickly."

Along with the soup we had opened a package of noodles with sauce and a package of vegetable protein that Isobel had cut into cubes and put into the noodles so Caroline could mix them up. Caroline brought the bowl to Irene and Eleanor used the tongs to put noodles onto Irene's plate, then Isobel used a spoon to pour more of the protein cubes and sauce on top. They did the same for Robbert and then brought the bowl to May.

"Would you like noodles, May?" asked Eleanor.

May nodded, watching Eleanor dig with the tongs and extract just the right amount of noodles, then push aside the noodles to make room for the spoon to get the sauce. When they were done, Caroline carried the bowl back to the countertop, and I held the pot for Isobel to ladle soup into their bowls.

"Would you like soup, May?" asked Isobel.

May nodded again. Her hands were in her lap, even though Robbert and Irene had gone ahead and started to eat. When we were done I carried the pot back to the stove, which was where it lived if someone still might decide on seconds. May stared at everything we did, and then at the kitchen around her.

But May wasn't eating.

"Where am I?" she whispered. "What is this place?"

Robbert put down his spoon and sniffed. He scraped his chair backward, just enough to cross his legs, and studied May, like she hadn't figured something out in class.

"No."

May looked up at him—not knowing how Robbert thought—since "no" wasn't strictly an answer to either of her questions. The four of us did know, of course, and though we wanted to help her, we'd learned it was best to stay quiet.

"Answer your own question, May," Robbert said. "Where are you? You're a stranger sharing our meal. I'm glad you're feeling better—good enough to go exploring despite being asked to do no such thing. I'm also glad because this means you feel good enough to answer some questions yourself."

May held still, like a lizard trying to hide. Irene nodded to Robbert, and her eyes were different than the softness in her words, as if they had silently decided something between them.

"Now, Robbert—" she began, but Robbert shook his head.

"I'm speaking to May, Irene. I think she owes us an explanation . . . *all* of us."

May swallowed and the swallowing bobbed her head, even though her eyes kept staring at her soup. I saw the stripe of freckles below her eyes and wondered if they'd always been a part of her face, or if they were like the scab—something no one had expected but that, from then on, she had to remember.

I walked to the counter, to where we cleared the table for dinner. By the time I crossed back to May everyone was looking at me. I set the zipped rubber pouch next to her plate.

"I found it with you, May. We looked at your pictures and

asked ourselves a lot of questions. But now that you're awake, we can all look together."

May pulled the bag onto her lap, one thumb rubbing back and forth along the zipper. She looked up at me. Her words got tangled.

"W-which—I'm sorry—I forgot your name."

"I'm Veronika. My hair is red. I found you."

"Veronika saved your life," said Robbert.

May looked down and squeezed the rubber bag. "Thank you."

"Can we look at your pictures?" I asked.

"May should eat something first," said Irene. "At least her soup."

Now May was sniffing. She wiped her nose on her fingers and then her fingers on her shorts. She leaned forward to eat. I stayed where I was, next to her, since I'd been the one to make her talk.

In the end May ate her noodles, too, and the table was cleared and wiped so nothing spilled could touch the pictures. We expected May to describe each one in turn, because that was what we did, but instead she unzipped the bag and looked through them all without talking. Eleanor was about to speak, just ahead of me wanting to speak, but Robbert put his hand on her shoulder. We were to wait, because this was something new. Usually this meant an unfamiliar bird or cloud—different, but belonging to a group we already knew. May was another different altogether. Her group was the group of girls, which had been our group, but her being in it changed everything. From now on we were us compared to her.

This was even more true when May began to talk.

"The *Mary* is our boat. I lived there since I can remember, with Will, my uncle Will, and then later with Cat, too—Cat is my other uncle, though he's not my real uncle, but the *Mary* needs two people who can sail. In another year I could make three. I can do almost everything. That's Cat."

She pointed to the smiling man who held the fish in the fifth picture. Irene pointed to the first picture, of the two men on the dock.

"Is one of these men your uncle Will?"

May shook her head. "Those are friends of Cat."

"Where do they live? Where is that?"

May sniffed. "Port Orange."

"That's quite a distance," said Robbert. "Do you live there, keep a berth? Is that where you have family?"

May only shook her head.

"Not everyone feels welcome in Port Orange any more, do they, Irene?"

"They'd feel welcome if they had family," Irene said. "If they had a school, or a church."

May shrugged and stared down at the pictures.

"Where else did you sail in the *Mary*?" Robbert asked. "What was the biggest place?"

"Will doesn't like us to talk. About any of that."

"Why not?"

"We like to be left alone."

"So do we," said Robbert. May nodded, as if his words meant something more. She wiped her nose on her sleeve, turning her face since the sleeve was short.

"We're traveling people. We take cargo and messages, and we catch fish."

"What about Tarawa?" Irene asked. "Were you ever there?"

May shook her head.

"Not ever?"

"Not for a long time."

"Since things changed?"

May shrugged, like she wasn't sure.

"Didn't the people in Port Orange make you to go to their school?" asked Robbert.

May shook her head. "Will and Cat said no."

"I didn't think they let anyone say no."

"I don't know. I guess I stayed out of sight below."

"When you took things for people, carried cargo, did you know what it was?" Irene pointed to the crates on the dock in the first picture. "Was it always things like this—this big? Or smaller?"

May thought about all the different crates. "Usually smaller."

"Did you know what was in them?"

"Will never let me."

"But you looked," said Irene. "Didn't you, May?"

May turned. She didn't answer at once. She was staring at Caroline's hair. "Sometimes books. Sometimes chips and wires. Or parts to make machines. Mostly we set up meets with other boats offshore—then go into port afterward, all empty, so a search didn't matter."

Irene and Robbert looked at each other. "Your uncle Will sounds very careful," said Robbert. "Everyone has to be careful these days, don't they, May?"

Isobel tugged at Robbert's sleeve. "Do you know May's uncle or his friend Cat?"

"Maybe the men on our supply boat know them," said Eleanor. "Maybe we can ask."

"Can you read, May?" asked Irene, not paying attention to Eleanor.

May shrugged.

"We read very well," said Eleanor.

"Is that your parrot?" asked Isobel, pointing.

"No."

"What happened to your finger?"

"I caught it on a fishhook."

"Why is your boat named *Mary*?"

"Mary was Will's mother. She died."

"Did she have an accident?"

"What happened in the storm?" asked Caroline.

Irene put a hand on Caroline's shoulder, because at that question May went still again.

"I don't know," she finally said. "I fell out of my bunk. It was dark, it was too noisy to hear. I fell into water—water in the cabin. I shouted for Will and Cat. I went on deck. I should have stayed below. I couldn't hear anyone. I didn't know. The swells were too big. I couldn't hang on."

"What are swells?" asked Eleanor, blinking. "What is deck"?

May sniffed.

"Swell is another word for wave," said Irene quietly. "Deck is the floor on a boat."

We all nodded, filling things in.

"Why did you have your bag?" I asked May.

"We might be sinking."

"Were you sinking?"

May shook her head. Her voice was soft. "I never saw. I wish I could have done something."

"Water is extremely dangerous for anyone," whispered Isobel.

• • •

Irene carried May back to the classroom. Even though everyone still had questions, May stopped being able to sit without yawning, like Robbert did at breakfast. Robbert stayed while we got ready for bed. We lay on our cots, a little worried that it wasn't Irene saying good night like usual, but for once Robbert wasn't in a hurry. He sat next to our folded smocks, with the light turned off, in a quiet that at first made us think he still had questions but then was only quiet by itself.

Very softly, I began to sing. The others sang with me, soft and clear, filling the room like moonlight.

> *A honeybee is born to roam*
> *To search for flowers sweet,*
> *Across the waves of whitest foam*
> *For just one blossom treat.*
>
> *No matter where it finds itself,*
> *A bee can find its home.*
> *A honeybee is very brave.*
> *It works so very hard,*
> *From birth until its honeyed grave*
> *The hive and Queen to guard.*

No matter where it finds itself,
A bee can find its home.

Our voices faded, leaving only the breeze outside. Irene stood in the doorway.

"I heard you singing. I thought you'd be asleep."

"We were waiting for you," said Robbert, and suddenly it seemed like we had been, all of us waiting to be together after such a busy day. Irene sat next to Robbert, listening with us to the night.

"What will happen now?" whispered Caroline. She was across the room in the dark. I thought about what Caroline knew, and what I didn't.

"We'll go to sleep," said Irene. She went to Caroline first, whispering in her ear. I wanted to hear what she said. I wanted to know if something had changed and, because inside I knew it had, whether we could change it back.

She came to me last, like always.

5.

The next morning Caroline woke having had a dream. While Eleanor tied my smock I watched Caroline sit with her head cocked to one side, staring at nothing. Irene knelt next to her, whispering quietly. Caroline stood, still caught in her thoughts, while Irene unfolded her smock. As she dressed her, Irene spoke to the rest of us, waiting patiently for Caroline to find her own way to being awake.

"I asked everyone to think about what we can do with the sailcloth in the yard. It will be dry by now, and I was hoping we could try some of your ideas."

She had Caroline's ties done and took her hand. Irene pointed with her chin at the kitchen and the three of us got going on breakfast, putting water in the kettle and measuring tea for the pot. Irene and Caroline stayed in the bedroom for another few minutes. When they finally came in Caroline was focused as ever, going straight to the cupboard for the oatmeal, which was what Irene had decided to cook.

"Will May have breakfast with us?" asked Eleanor, setting the table.

"Not this morning," said Irene. "She's still asleep."

Isobel asked how much May slept normally versus how much she slept now and whether that was a question of living on a boat or nearly drowning or the yellow pills. While Irene answered, I noticed Caroline looking at me. Eleanor asked Irene about May's bandages, how many there had been before versus how many she had now and which ones would be the last to come off, or would there be some that never did, and also about the scab on the side of May's face.

"What did you dream?" I asked, deciding to whisper. Caroline shook her head.

"Veronika?"

I turned to Irene, because I'd also been listening to them. "My idea was to make an awning for shade on the kitchen porch."

"That's very good," she said. "Caroline?"

"My idea was about water." Irene looked at her, as if she didn't quite understand, so Caroline went on. "To stretch the canvas and catch water when it rains, to store it, to make tea."

"That's very good, too. It's already a good morning, with all of you being so smart." We always wanted to make Irene happy, and she smiled as she sat down to eat. "Caroline, why don't you go ask Robbert if he has anything we can use to cut the sailcloth. Be careful not to disturb anyone."

We all watched as Caroline walked out and carefully went down the steps and across the yard, though she was only part-way across when Irene called us away from the door to plan the rest of the morning. We had so many ideas, and she had so many questions, that we barely noticed Caroline didn't come back.

Eventually we took a nap—which was when we finally realized how long she'd been away—but when we woke up Caroline was there with the rest of us like always. Irene had eaten her lunch while we were sleeping, so we went straight into the yard. Irene explained our walk would be without minutes, with all of us walking together. The difference, she said, was that this time we wouldn't be walking alone. She pointed and we saw May on the porch of Robbert's building. The shape of her face had changed, because her hair was pulled behind her head. She had borrowed one of Irene's clips. We never used Irene's clips, because we needed our hair like it was, hanging down and wiped clean to catch the sun. Irene waved for May to join us.

"We're all going to walk together," she said, and then to May, "We can show May our island."

Irene held out her hands to Eleanor and to Isobel. "And no pinching," said Isobel.

"That's right," said Irene, with a smile, still looking at May. Caroline and I stood with May. Usually the two not holding hands with Irene just waited to hold hands with her on the walk back. But now we were with May, who just looked down at her feet. Since I had done it before, I reached to touch May's hand. She pulled back, surprised.

"We hold hands with Irene," said Caroline.

"O," said May, but nothing else.

Caroline held out her hand. May looked at it, then over at Irene, who was watching everything.

"Why did she say 'no pinching'?"

"Because we don't pinch," said Caroline.

"That's right," I said, just like Irene. I held out my hand, too. May finally took it and then took Caroline's.

"We're off then," said Irene. "Isobel, where first?"

"The cliffs," said Isobel.

"Why the cliffs? Eleanor?"

"Because we'll see more, since the tide is out."

"Very good." Irene dipped her eyes once right at me, a hidden look, and then turned to lead the way.

May wasn't as good at walking with us as Irene, so there was some stumbling, which meant that the three of us fell behind, just enough that—as May realized first—we could talk without the others hearing.

"Are you . . . okay now?"

May's voice was still a little hoarse, scraped in her throat. She was looking at Caroline. Caroline didn't answer, blinking, and it seemed like May wasn't sure what to say next, or even what words to use, like she'd met a bird or a flower that didn't have a name. She tried again.

"He . . . Robbert . . . this morning . . . he was . . . working . . . on you—"

"Robbert wanted to know about my dream," said Caroline, just as softly as May. She looked ahead to see if Irene had heard—she hadn't—then across to me. Caroline knew this walk was about our learning to see what May saw, another version of an island we already knew. That meant paying attention to May. But since now there were things Caroline wasn't supposed to talk about—and maybe this morning's dream was one of them, too—she had to decide which task was more important. The easiest thing, since I didn't have the rules she had, was to do some deciding for her.

"Caroline has dreams, May. None of the rest of us do."

"Why not?" asked May. Her voice was blunt. "And how can you have dreams?"

"I don't," I said.

"But how can *one* of you have them when you're all the same?"

"We aren't the same. We have different hair."

May just made a face like hair didn't count.

We've done different things," I said.

"Like what?"

"Like deciding to stay longer on a walk. Like deciding at all."

May made another face. "Everyone decides."

"Not always," I said. "Isobel and Eleanor and Caroline didn't decide like I did, just like Isobel and Eleanor and I don't have dreams. Just like they didn't find you. I found you, and that was another decision. Caroline doesn't know what that was. And Caroline found something on the beach. I don't know about that."

May turned to Caroline, blunt again. "What did you find? What was it?"

Caroline was stuck between different rules. "I don't know," she finally whispered. "I didn't know what it was."

May glanced at Irene. "Did they know?"

Caroline nodded.

"Was it the same thing in your dream?" I asked.

Caroline didn't answer.

"Was it?" May demanded, pulling at Caroline's hand. Caroline nodded.

"Why don't they want you to say?"

"Sometimes that's the way we learn. Things have correct sequences, and if one comes too soon we have to wait."

"But this is happening now."

May's voice had become loud enough for Irene to look back. I waved at her. May looked down at her feet until Irene looked away, then whispered to me.

"And you can't dream."

"I don't, whether I can't or not. But Caroline does."

May shook her head. "No, she doesn't. She's doing something else."

Since I really wanted to know what Caroline had seen, instead of answering May, I waited. Just like she had before, May shifted the question.

"What did you dream?" she asked Caroline.

Caroline blinked, because she felt May's hands squeezing and heard the changes in May's voice. Since I was on the side of May's face with the scab, I could also watch the skin being pulled when she spoke, tight on the curve of her cheek.

"I don't know it's a dream when it happens," said Caroline. "I only wake up slow, slow from remembering. When I put that memory next to others I see it doesn't fit inside my time, that the dream is out of order, like making oatmeal in the middle of a walk."

"But are the dreams memories? Real things that happened?"

"Not always. But now they seem like mine."

"But how? Where can they come from?"

"Irene says dreams are different thinking. Where do your dreams come from?"

"My dreams aren't like *that*," May said. "When *I* dream I don't need anyone to—to—what *he* was doing. No one does."

"What was your dream this morning?" I asked Caroline.

"I was listening to Robbert."

May frowned. "What was he saying?"

"He was telling me to hide."

Eleanor called back to be careful, because the first person to reach the cliffs always let everyone else know we were near the edge. Actually it wasn't hard to tell, since the black rock extended at least ten yards back from the lip. When you reached the band of black, it was time to watch out.

Being on the cliffs was like being on the dock or on the beach—it was a place you could only go if you knew how to keep away from danger. There was a spot where we stood to look out, a good safe distance back since Robbert had explained how rock can crumble, how gravel was slippery, and how sur-faces can't be trusted.

We caught up to the others at the lookout spot. The cliff curved on either side, so you could see all the way to the water, which meant you could also see the seaweed, the crabs, the birds, the nests, the barnacles, and the waves. Irene took her hands from Isobel and Eleanor and tucked hair the wind had pulled free behind her ear.

"How are your feet, May?"

"They're fine."

"Good. What did you see on your way? Did you girls show May how we take walks?"

"We study things," said Isobel. "As much as possible."

"They did." May nodded and looked at the ground, making it seem like she was shy about talking instead of the truth, which was that she hadn't looked at all. Irene turned to Eleanor, for a good example.

"What did you see, Eleanor?"

Eleanor described the wind, how it had strengthened as we'd come closer to the cliffs, and how the direction had changed in little ways as the path wound up the slope. She pointed to the water and explained how the wind was connected to the tide, and how the tide determined, for just one example, what all the seabirds were doing.

May shaded her eyes with one hand and pointed farther up the cliffs. "What's up there?"

We all followed her gaze, and saw—because we saw Irene nodding—that May was showing us something about ourselves. The crest of the hill, in fact the highest point on the island, wasn't the cliffs proper—they were only the highest spot where we could safely climb. The island itself rose for another hundred yards, above the grass and trees, to a crumbling spike of red stone. The ledges were spattered white from birds, and they flew around the peak in patterns that, just like the waves, would entrance us if we stared too hard—wide loops of numbers in the air, swinging and falling until we lost track of anything else. Instead of looking at the peak, we had learned to focus simply on the path and then on the cliffs when we reached them. So when May pointed up we all looked with her, but just as quickly dropped our eyes away.

"That's the peak," said Isobel.

"Has anyone climbed it?" asked May.

"It's very high," said Eleanor. "And extremely dangerous."

"It's just as bad as water," said Caroline.

May kept looking up. She pointed again. "What is *that*?"

Her finger picked out a spiked metal pole that rose from a squat steel box that had been bolted to the rock.

"That's Robbert's aerial," I said. "For the satellites."

May turned to me, with her mouth crooked. "So *he* can climb."

"It's extremely dangerous," repeated Eleanor.

"Looks like it," May agreed. She hobbled forward, to stand with Irene and the others, but then all at once she darted past, right up to the cliff edge.

"May—" began Irene.

But May was already sitting on the lip and dangling both legs down.

"May!" Caroline was shouting, and I was shouting with her. "Come back!"

"What are you scared of?" May looked over her shoulder with a grin. "Nothing's going to happen . . . or is it?" Then she suddenly lurched, like she was about to launch herself into the air. As we all started to scream we saw she hadn't jumped after all—that it was a joke, because May was laughing, laughing at us.

"That's enough, May."

Irene walked to her, closer to the edge than any of us had ever seen Irene go, and took May's hand, pulling her up. May came along, still smiling, but now to herself, like it was something no one else understood.

On the way down Caroline and I walked with Irene, so there was no more talk of dreams. We barely talked at all, mainly because Irene was thinking, and when we did talk—when she asked us a question—she didn't ask a second one afterward, like usual. This gave Caroline and me time to think, too, glancing across Irene, me about what I didn't know and Caroline about what she did. But both of us also thought about May and the edge of the cliff, and about the peak. The truth was, we never did think of the peak, simply because we'd been taught not to—almost as if we'd been taught not to even *see* it, though we caught glimpses of it all the time. I glanced over my shoulder and there it was behind the palms, the red stone sharp against the sky. Irene squeezed my hand.

"Just because she's foolish enough to go to the edge doesn't mean you should. I hope you know that."

She thought I'd looked back at May.

"I don't want to go to the edge," I said, and then so she wouldn't be worried, "That rule is there for a reason."

"And it's our business to be careful," said Caroline.

"It is," agreed Irene.

"Is May not careful because she was hurt?" asked Caroline. "Because of the ocean?"

"Or is it because she's different?"

I watched Irene for an answer. Irene glanced at May and the others, who had fallen even farther behind, and lowered her voice, as if she were giving Caroline and me special instructions.

"Everyone is different—"

"We're not," said Caroline.

"It's impolite to interrupt, Caroline. And you *are* different. Just not in as many ways as May."

"But our differences are shared," I said. "In school."

Irene sighed. "Are they, Veronika? Always?"

"No."

"Then why did you say they were?"

"Because that's the rule."

"And what's a rule when it's broken?"

"A problem to be solved," said Caroline. "Like me."

"No," said Irene. "No. A person is not a problem."

"But when I have dreams—"

"You aren't a problem, Caroline."

"Is May?" I asked.

"Of course not." Irene squeezed our hands. "She's only a girl."

We spent the rest of the day helping Robbert cut the canvas sail, some of us measuring, and others holding the cloth to make it easier to use the shears. There was enough canvas for all of our ideas—an awning, a rain trap, window shades, and a runner for the porch steps to stop splinters—with the girl whose idea was being cut standing next to Robbert to watch closely. May stood with Irene, since she hadn't had an idea. Isobel asked if she had imagined so many things could be made from her sail. May shook her head and then Irene suggested another walk, and the two of them went alone toward the dock. I wondered if May would dangle her legs off the dock, too—if Irene would let her or pull her away, or if going there at all was a test to see if May had learned. I hoped she had.

When they returned we were already in the kitchen because that night Robbert was cooking. He didn't do things the same as Irene, so we had to look sharp, which was what he called out whenever he caught one of us waiting without a job. "Look sharp!" he would shout, and whoever he shouted at had to be ready. Irene came in by herself, explaining before anyone could ask that May was having her own nap and might eat with us or might not, since sleep was important for her getting better. Isobel poured a cup of water for Irene from the filter. Irene took a big drink and scooted her chair to the cupboards and looked inside, nodding her chin as she counted the boxes and cans.

"How long until the boat comes?" asked Eleanor. We knew Irene hadn't opened the peanut butter, so for her to be counting cans seemed soon.

"That's a good question," Irene replied. She shut the cupboard and held out her cup for Isobel to refill. "But who can tell me something else, something about May's pictures?"

"What about them?" I asked, before anyone. "Which one?"

We all stopped what we doing and looked for the photographs. They weren't on the table anymore. Had they been given back to May? Should we go wake her up? Caroline was two steps to the door before Robbert told her to wait. He wiped his hands and cleared a space at the table. From his satchel on the floor he took his black notebook and set it where everyone could see. He tapped a button and all seven of May's pictures were there, each one a little box. Robbert tapped again and the entire screen was filled with the first picture, the sunny dock piled with crates and the two smiling men.

"Those are friends of Cat," said Eleanor. "Cat is like May's uncle except not her real uncle. Will is her real uncle. Cat is his friend. Will's mother was Mary, which is the name of the boat. This photograph was taken from the deck of the *Mary*."

"Very good," said Irene. "What about the crates?"

"There are seventy-four of them," said Isobel. "Five main sizes make up fifty-nine crates and fifteen other sizes are one crate each."

"Do you see any writing?"

The crates had all kinds of writing but the actual letters were hard to see because of the grain of the photograph.

"I see 'Orange,'" I said.

"For Port Orange," said Eleanor. "I see 'volume' and 'kilo' and 'mhz' and numbers. One number is 805324776."

She pointed at that crate. Since everyone saw numbers, we all began to call them out until Irene raised her hand.

"Like a tree full of parrots," she said. "One at a time. What else?"

"Is there something we're supposed to find first?" I asked.

"No. But your eyes are better than ours."

"Because you're old," Isobel said to Robbert. "You say your eyes are old and then you rub them."

"Where is *that*?" Caroline pointed to a gap between two piles of crates. Beyond the gap was a dark band, thicker than the horizon line of the ocean.

"Isn't it a shadow?" said Irene, looking at Robbert. He took off his glasses and leaned closer, to squint.

"Is it?" he asked, looking at us.

"It's land," said Eleanor. "Far away and high up, like our cliffs."

"Port Orange doesn't have cliffs anywhere near it," said Robbert. "Nothing like that elevation."

"May must have made a mistake," Isobel suggested. "Because of her injury."

But Robbert wasn't listening. He tapped the screen and we saw the second photograph, the green island across the water, wreathed with fog and clouds, and then the fourth picture, from the beach out to the sea. He tapped again and again, switching back and forth between them, frowning. Irene watched him.

"Robbert—"

"We have to know for sure."

"But if she can't tell us—"

"Or won't."

"Well—exactly."

He spun the notebook to face Irene, but she only tightened her lips.

"Surely it's time to eat." Irene crossed to the counter and took over from Robbert as if she'd been cooking all along. We all went to help and soon it was dinner like normal, with Irene asking us about tomorrow's weather.

But weather only made me think of the fog around May's island—hers only because she'd captured it in a picture, not because she lived there, though maybe she actually did, or had. Anything was possible if what she said wasn't reliable: which was what Robbert thought, if the dock with the crates wasn't in Port Orange after all. I knew he wondered if the island in the other pictures was the same island with the dock, and that he was switching back and forth to identify it precisely. I didn't know why that was important because I didn't know why May was unreliable. When we didn't say something it was because we didn't know, or because no one asked the right way. May was more like Robbert or Irene, who didn't say things for their own reasons, but I thought of Caroline not being able to talk about her dreams and wondered if May couldn't talk because Will or Cat had given her instructions.

"Are you sure May isn't hungry?" I asked.

Robbert had his chopsticks halfway to his open mouth. He paused, leaving them in the air, noodles dripping sauce, then set them back in his bowl.

"You're right, Veronika. You're absolutely right. Come here."

"Robbert, we can't keep pressing," said Irene.

"I know we can't." Robbert had picked up his satchel and reached inside, using both hands to fiddle with something I couldn't see that snapped and clicked. He zipped the satchel and looped it over my shoulder. Then he scooped the rest of the noodles into a plastic bowl and stabbed another pair of chopsticks in so they stuck up like a bug's antennae. He held out the bowl for me to take with both hands, then went to open the door. Irene never moved, and the other three just watched.

"Off you go, Veronika," Robbert said. "Make sure to set the satchel down on the floor when you go in, and then bring it back when you're done. Do you understand?"

"Yes, Robbert."

"And make sure May eats the noodles. Stay there and talk until she's done. Ask her questions."

"What if she's asleep?"

That was Irene. Robbert knelt next to me. "Then Veronika should wake her."

Irene sighed. "Gently, Veronika. Don't frighten her. Just say her name or very softly touch her arm. And if she doesn't wake up right away, you come back."

"And no whispering," said Robbert. "May is your friend. Don't be shy."

I walked carefully not to drop the chopsticks, especially climbing the classroom steps with no hands. I saw May's shadow through the screen.

"Who is it?" she asked in her raspy voice. "Which one of you?"

"It's Veronika," I said, trying to speak loudly. "I brought you dinner."

"What is it?"

"Peanut noodles with protein strips and kelp."

"Leave it there."

"I'm supposed to make sure you eat it, because you have to recover."

"I'm fine."

"Not your feet."

"Feet don't matter."

"What if you fall down? What if you're on the cliff?"

May snorted through her nose. "Where's everyone else?"

"Eating."

May snorted again. "Or *not* eating."

"If they're finished. Then they're cleaning up, or maybe Irene will ask us to sing."

May's voice went soft again. "I heard you last night."

"Can I come in?" I asked.

May opened the door with its wheezing hinge. "I'll come out," she said. "We can look at the stars."

I sat next to May on the top step and gave her the noodles. I put the satchel between my feet.

"What's that?" asked May, with her mouth full.

"Robbert's satchel."

"Why do you have it?"

"He asked me to bring it back to him."

"What's in it?"

"I don't know."

"Don't you want to look?"

"No."

May wrinkled her nose. She looked at the bowl and stirred the noodles into a ball. "Why did they send you?"

"I asked if you were hungry."

"How long have you been here? This place, without anyone knowing?"

I didn't understand what May's question had to do with being hungry, but I told her that we'd been on the island for as long as we could remember, and then about the accidental plane crash and our parents. May snorted and at first I thought she'd choked but then I saw her shake her head, which shook her hair. She was smiling.

"It isn't funny, May."

"What?" It was like she hadn't heard me.

"It isn't funny," I repeated, firmly. "Being an orphan is very hard." She didn't answer. It was important, so I went on. "We girls are very lucky to have Irene and Robbert. We are lucky to have a home, and a school, and lucky to have each other. If we didn't, where do you think we'd be?"

I heard my loud voice echo across the yard. May didn't say anything, like she hadn't even listened.

"Where would *you* be?" I asked.

"You girls," May whispered.

I waited for her to say more. Instead she kept rolling the ball of noodles in the bowl. The smell attracted insects, flitting around May's head.

"When Robbert asks questions it can be hard," I said.

Then she turned to face me with a different voice. "How is it hard for *you*?"

"Because he knows what we're supposed to say."

"I hate that," said May.

"That doesn't make him not know. It doesn't change what you're supposed to learn."

"I'm not here to *learn*."

"What else would you do?"

"Talk to a tree." May put the bowl down and watched the insects settle, then pushed it so they rose in a cloud. "Talk to you."

"I'm not a tree."

"You're not a girl."

"I'm not your kind of girl."

"I'm the only kind."

"Not here. And there are more of us than you." I stood up, slipped the satchel over my shoulder, and bent down for her bowl. "I'm sorry for your feet, May, and for your boat, and your uncle, and your uncle's friend Cat. I'm sorry you're an orphan."

I walked down the steps, the bowl in both hands. Behind me May stomped back inside and slammed the screen.

"You don't even know where this is!" she cried. "You don't even know!"

Ahead of me I could see shapes in the kitchen doorway, and I knew May was wrong. For the first time I understood that Robbert and Irene were like the rest of us, orphans, too.

6.

The next morning Robbert wasn't there for breakfast. Afterward, when we sat on the porch while Irene drank her tea, Isobel pointed between the two buildings. Just visible in the distance was Robbert, coming down the path. We waved, even though he wasn't looking in our direction.

"Has Robbert been walking to the cliffs?" asked Eleanor.

"Maybe he has," Irene replied. "It's a lovely morning."

"Will we walk to the cliffs, too?" asked Eleanor.

The screen door squeaked and May stepped onto the classroom porch. She was wearing what she'd worn when I'd found her, canvas shorts and a black shirt with buttons down the middle. Most of the buttons had been pulled off in the water, but May had replaced them with pins. Her feet were still bandaged and in the flip-flops.

I knew she'd been upset the night before, so I waved and called out. "Good morning, May!"

Everyone else waved, too, but May didn't wave back. She came down the steps and across the yard. When she got to the foot of our steps she stopped, possibly because we stood in a row across the top and there was no clear path.

"Good morning, May," said Irene. "How did you sleep?"

"Well, thank you." May's voice was still raspy. Since the rest of her seemed better, I wondered if it was always raspy. "And I guess I'm hungry."

"Then you should eat," said Caroline.

May acted like she hadn't heard, and spoke to Irene. "Where is Robbert?"

"He's right there," Irene said, and she pointed. By now Robbert had reached the meadow. This time he saw us and waved his left hand. His right carried his red toolbox. Irene stood and brushed off the seat of her skirt. "Come on in, May. Let's all whip up a meal."

"I want to talk to Robbert," May said.

"About what?" Isobel asked.

May didn't answer. Irene put a hand on Isobel's shoulder. "Don't be rude, May."

May kicked her flip-flop against the canvas runner that now covered the steps. "That's my sail," she said.

Robbert came into the courtyard. He saw us standing together, saw May looking at him, and waved again. Without a word, though, he kept going into the classroom.

When I'd come back with May's unfinished noodles the night before, Robbert had taken his satchel away. Now it lay on the countertop, unzipped and shoved to the side, yawning like a big soft clam. Inside lay Robbert's notebook, but not whatever else had been there the night before, what he had reached inside to click. Was the click to put something to sleep or wake it up? Then I wondered why he hadn't taken the notebook back to the classroom where it usually lived and decided Irene wanted to use it. When Robbert used the notebook the lines were short and broken and would scroll and hop when he pushed the button. When Irene used it we saw pictures and words.

As it turned out, Irene hadn't eaten all the oatmeal we'd made, so it was easy to heat the rest and serve it hot to May. May also drank some of Irene's tea, in a cup we almost never used, like Irene's but dusty and needing a wash. May kept looking over her shoulder, like she wanted to leave or like she wanted someone to arrive. Then she noticed Robbert's satchel.

"What's that?"

"Robbert's satchel," said Eleanor.

May looked at me, to let me know that she'd seen it before. "No, inside."

"Robbert's notebook," said Eleanor. "He and Irene use it for working."

"Does it connect?" asked May.

"Connect to what?"

May stared at Eleanor and her voice got hard. "Why are there four of you? Why does anyone need *four*?"

"Because we're the same," said Eleanor. "And because we're not."

"Some do tests," said Caroline. "And some do control."

"Do you do tests?" asked Isobel.

May didn't say anything, then shook her head. "Tests is school."

"May," said Irene, with a deliberate slowness that told you to get ready. "How do you tell time?"

May stared again at Eleanor. "What do you mean?"

"What do you *use*? On the boat. A watch? Navigation instruments? The sun?"

"You can't always see the sun," said Isobel.

May was still frowning. "Will had an old watch, with hands. The boat clocks used numbers. But Cat taught me to use the sun. We would do it every day at noon."

"You can't always see the sun," repeated Isobel.

"We would make measurements anyway, and write them down. We would compare them to what we found the next time we did see the sun. And we had the boat clock anyway." May's voice had become tighter. She swallowed some tea and turned to Isobel. "How do you do it? Do you just *know*?"

"Know what?"

"What time it is."

"Yes," Isobel replied, though that didn't answer whatever question May was trying to ask. "Just like everyone."

May didn't say anything, and after a moment Eleanor took May's empty bowl and put it in the sink. May saw Caroline waiting, then finished her tea and put the cup in Caroline's hands. Isobel collected the spoon. There wasn't anything for me to collect, so I told May that I hoped she enjoyed her oatmeal. May glanced again at Robbert's satchel, so I glanced with her. The only thing there was the notebook.

May pushed back her chair with a scrape, but I was still looking at the satchel, blinking because I realized that the thin edge of the notebook, which I'd never had any reason to notice, was lined with numbers, and one set of numbers was 805324776, which Eleanor had seen the night before printed on a crate, which meant that more notebooks like Robbert's had been inside.

"Well," said Irene, standing. "I think it's time for a very special walk."

• • •

The six of us, Robbert still not having reappeared, stood at the edge of the grassy dunes facing the beach. The tide was coming in, but the upper part of the beach remained dry and firm. The wind was fresh and strong, blowing our hair and whipping May's even more. Irene called over the sound.

"Since we were talking of time, we're going to do an experiment. Instead of setting a time limit, I'm going to let you all decide how long your walk should be—as long as, when you get back, you're able to tell me why. Now, some of you go this way." Irene pointed up the beach in the direction I'd found May. "And some of you go the other."

We looked at Irene, wanting her to decide, but she only clapped her hands, which was the signal to set off. No one moved, not even May, who stood with her fists in the pockets of her shorts. Irene motioned to Isobel. Isobel went to her and Irene whispered into Isobel's ear. When she was done, Isobel walked past the rest of us and down the beach. Irene did the same to Eleanor, and Eleanor set off in the same direction as Isobel, and then Caroline, but Caroline went the opposite way, up the beach toward the grassy dunes. Then she motioned to me.

"This will be like last night on the steps," she whispered. "You need to walk with May and remember what she says. And you need to catch up to Caroline and make sure she doesn't fall."

I wanted to ask why Caroline would fall any more than I would, but Irene was already patting my shoulder and turning me around. "You go with Veronika, May, since you two are friends."

May snorted and started away by herself. I followed, and even though she walked much closer to the water than I could, so we couldn't really talk—even kicking her flip-flops through the foam, which I knew was bad for her bandages—May kept her pace slow enough that we stayed together.

But since Irene had told me talking was important, I finally stopped. May went a few more yards, as if she hadn't seen, but then stopped, too. She dropped to a crouch, picking at some dead coral.

"Isn't there something you're supposed to *do*?" she called, still not looking at me. "Something you have to *learn*?"

I nodded.

"Then why don't you go *learn* it?" May stood, having pried the lump of coral from the sand. She flung it with both hands at an approaching wave, breaking the glassy curl of water. The tumble of foam halted just short of May's toes.

I took three steps closer to her, making sure the sand was still dry.

"I'm not your *friend*," said May, squatting again and speaking to the sand.

Eleanor and Isobel were out of sight, beyond the beach's turn. Ahead was Caroline, moving slowly, but widening the gap since we'd stopped. I couldn't see Irene at all.

"I would like you to be," I called.

"Why? What does it matter?" May pried out another piece of coral, dripping sand. She looked at me and then with a sudden jerk heaved the coral in my direction. It landed with a thump a yard short, kicking up sand, then rolled back toward the water.

"What do you think happened to your uncle Will and his friend Cat?" I asked.

May snorted again. "I think they're dead."

"But why?"

"Why?"

"I'm sorry you're sad, May."

"Shut up about it. Are you stupid?"

"I'm not stupid, May. I'm asking whether it was a storm or something else. But you don't know, do you? Because you were asleep."

"There was a storm."

"I know."

"So what else could it be?"

"That's what I was wondering."

"Why?"

"Because of everything, May. Because you said the picture

was Port Orange when it was somewhere else. Because the cargo on the *Mary* was things like Robbert's notebook."

May sniffed. "So what?"

"We're all together now, May. What anybody knows should be for everyone." But even as I spoke, I knew this wasn't true.

"They don't tell *you* everything."

"Robbert and Irene tell us as much as we can understand. We learn in pieces, and then we put the pieces together—"

"But you don't know where he was this *morning*, do you?" May had a smile, but it wasn't happy.

"Robbert went for a walk."

"Who goes on a walk with a toolbox? He went to the aerial!"

I had to admit that I couldn't remember Robbert ever walking with the toolbox, and I couldn't think of anything else near the cliffs that would require it. "Was the aerial broken?"

"Don't be so stupid!"

"I'm not stupid, May."

"You think they're so good!"

"Of course I do."

May turned away, out to the water. I glanced where she was looking to make sure she hadn't seen anything in particular— like a boat or something floating—and then looked down at May's feet, half sunk in the wet sand.

"They saved your life, May. We all did."

The wind pulled May's hair in black curling streamers. Caroline had vanished around the curve. I remembered what Irene had told me.

"I have to find Caroline, May."

I began to walk. I hadn't even reached the driest sand when I heard May's footsteps behind me, slapping wet, and then suddenly it hit me and I fell forward hard. I tried to extend my arms but there wasn't time, and my face hit the sand with a smack.

I lay there, blinking, sand stuck to my face. I couldn't get my arms underneath to push myself up. I couldn't move.

"May!" I called. "May!"

But May didn't answer.

"Caroline!" But Caroline was too far away, too far to even see what had happened. Irene should have sent her to look after me. I angled my head to the water. A wave broke toward me, the foam rushing up the sand. It stopped well away, but I knew the waves would just get higher. In half an hour the foam would touch my feet. Would Caroline come back in half an hour? Would she come back the same way? What if May had run to Caroline instead of going back? What if they went home through the dunes and left me?

I shook my head. I had been hit in two places on my back— two hands. What if May pushed Caroline down as well?

I tried to raise my knee but only dug it deeper. I lifted with my arms but my hands were pinned too far back, and it only drove my face into the sand. I called again, for May, for Caroline, for anyone who could hear.

The waves came closer, bit by bit, drawing back and tumbling forward. I realized I was staring and shut my eyes. How long had I stared? I turned away, blinking. The beach was a slope. I remembered May's coral, landing at my feet and rolling back.

I rocked my body up the hill and then toward the surf. Was I too heavy? What if I couldn't stop and rolled right into the water? But I did it again and again. Each time I rolled a little more, even though each time also dug me deeper in the sand.

At the height of the roll I stabbed my hand out, catching my body, just balanced with my back to the rising water. I pushed, just a little more, and dredged my knee from its trough of sand. I lifted with that arm and leg and rose enough to shift my other hand. I pushed again and got the other leg beneath me and then very carefully, sand sliding from my limbs, I managed to stand.

May wasn't anywhere I could see. I walked as quickly as I could to find Caroline.

Caroline stood in the dunes, watching the wind go through the grass. She looked up when I called, and watched for the time it took me to get near.

"You're all sandy," she said. "Did you fall? Did May help you? Where is she?"

"May pushed me down," I said.

"Why?"

"May is unhappy."

Caroline studied me closely. "That was very dangerous!"

"I thought she might have come here."

"To push me, too?"

"I didn't know."

"But you're the one who found her."

"I asked her what happened to Will and Cat."

"What did she say?"

"That they were dead."

"That doesn't mean what happened."

I nodded. "Robbert went to the aerial this morning, with the toolbox."

"Was it broken?"

"She said Irene and Robbert don't tell us things."

Caroline cocked her head. "They don't."

I told Caroline about the number on Robbert's notebook.

"Do Robbert and Irene know?" she asked.

"They must."

We stood without talking and then, even though we weren't walking, Caroline reached out and took my hand.

"You should tell me what you found on the beach," I said.

"I will," Caroline said. "But May is coming."

She walked to within five feet of where we stood and stopped. Caroline kept hold of my hand. The wind had pulled May's hair completely loose, and it flew around her head in a cloud, but underneath I saw her face had changed and her eyes were red and wet. She crossed her arms and, ducking her face like a bird, wiped her nose on her shoulder.

"I'm sorry," she said.

"What you did was extremely dangerous!" Caroline's voice was a shout.

"I know you're unhappy, May," I said.

May sniffed and rubbed her eye. "I came back but you were gone. I'm sorry. Don't tell them. Don't tell or they'll hate me even more."

"No one hates you, May."

"Unless you keep pushing people!" Caroline cried. "Because that is very serious!"

"I'm sorry. I'm really, really sorry."

May sank into a squat and hugged her knees.

"Then why did you push Veronika? Veronika found you."

"I don't know."

"Then you have to ask yourself very hard." Caroline's voice

was more quiet. "You have to know. And not be scared. There's nothing here to be scared of. We're not scared."

May looked up, but her eyes were far away.

"We need to help each other, May," I said. "We won't say anything to Irene."

"In exchange for what?" May's words were hesitant, like she wasn't sure if this was the answer—an answer we would understand—but hoped it was. But I understood her offer of an exchange to be an equation, a balance. "All right," I agreed. "We won't say anything, and then you will do something for us."

"What?"

"You'll tell us if anything happens when we're asleep."

May stood and looked at me and then at Caroline, who nodded. May nodded, too, all three of us making a deal. I held out my other hand.

"Just a minute." May hiked up her shirt and balled it over her fingers. "You're still covered in sand."

When we got back to the beach path, Irene was crouched with Isobel and Eleanor over the grass. Irene saw us coming and stood, taking Isobel's hand.

"We found a bird!" Eleanor called.

We gathered round: a dead gull, its feathers stuck together, stained and slick.

"It's a year old," Caroline said to Irene, and Irene nodded to let Caroline know that she was correct and also that Isobel or Eleanor had already said this.

"Look." Isobel gently flipped the gull to its other side, the soft neck lolling. "We found it high up, almost to the grass."

The other side of the gull was burned, feathers blackened and curled, the stubbled skin beneath blistered red.

"With the flotsam from the storm," said Eleanor, looking at May, as if she might have something to add.

But May only said, "Poor bird."

"How can a bird get burned?" I asked. "What can be on fire in a storm?"

We waited for Irene to explain. She stood with her hands in the pockets of her skirt. She took a deep breath, which she sometimes did standing in the wind—because of the fresh air, then she would let it all out with a smile. This time it came out through her nose.

"Who can answer Veronika's question? What burns?"

"Everything burns," said Eleanor. "But not in water. Not in rain."

"Something could burn and go into the rain afterward," said Isobel. "Something set on fire inside, where it's dry, and then thrown outside."

"The gull flew inside and then flew out again," suggested Eleanor.

"Inside where?" asked Caroline. "There's no fire here to burn a bird."

"Maybe it floated here on the tide," said Eleanor.

"But when?" asked Irene.

"During the storm," said Isobel. "This is the high-water mark."

"It could have been burned somewhere else," said Eleanor, "and during the storm it came here."

"How long has it been dead?" said Irene, in the way that meant this was a clue.

We saw things being dead all the time, mainly crabs and insects, but also birds and eggs and jellyfish. The gull hadn't begun to fall apart or even smell, and its feathers were still intact. I flipped it back to the side we'd first seen.

"What is that, all over its feathers?"

"Oil." Everyone looked at May. "Probably diesel."

"What is diesel?" asked Eleanor.

"It's fuel for the engine of a boat," said Irene, when May didn't answer.

"Uncle Will's boat?" asked Eleanor. "But May didn't say anything about a fire. Was there a fire, May? Was there a bird inside your boat?"

"Of course not," said May. She stood up and stepped away. "I don't know. I didn't see any fire. I don't know what happened to a stupid bird."

I stood up, too, wanting her to come back.

"I doubt a seagull was inside the boat," said Irene.

"Then how did it burn in the rain?" asked Isobel. "Was it inside *another* boat?"

"Seagulls aren't like parrots," said Irene. "You know that. Think again. May, what do you remember about when you woke up."

May turned to her, the wind whipping her hair across her eyes. "I don't remember anything."

"Did you see anyone?"

May shook her head.

"You called out for your uncle. For Cat. Didn't you? But they didn't answer."

"I wasn't loud enough."

"What woke you up, May? Was it a crash? A big bang?"

"I don't know."

Irene turned to the rest of us. "What do *you* think?" Her voice was impatient, but also something else. We almost never heard it—and only when Irene forgot we were awake or thought we couldn't hear—and that was her being sad, wanting something that she couldn't name. "What do you think, Caroline?"

Caroline blinked and cocked her head. "The oil."

"The oil caught fire!" said Eleanor quickly. "And the oil got all over the bird."

"And the rain put it out," said Isobel. "But by then the bird couldn't fly."

"And what started the fire," Eleanor pointed with her hand, "is what woke up May."

Everyone looked at May, but this time she looked back. She pulled the hair from her face and put it behind one ear. "When I woke up, the *Mary* was sinking. It was dark. I didn't see any fire. I didn't see anything. And you don't know. All of you, from a bird, you don't know. You don't know why anything!"

I went to May, close enough to see her lip shaking. I wondered if this was how she'd looked when she decided to push me down. Would she push me again, in front of everyone? I didn't think so, but I realized how little I understood her. If one of us had done what she had, pushing me, and then admitted it was wrong and made a deal, like with Caroline and me, that would be how we behaved from then on—but already May was back where she had been, feeling too many things at once and every agreement forgotten.

"What happened already did," I said to her. "Robbert says that if we understand the first accident, it stops a second one. If we know what happened to the *Mary* then it will help you when you get your own boat later on."

"We want to help you, May," said Eleanor.

"And we need you to help us." Irene's voice was the same mix of sharp and sad, but louder because of the wind, almost a call. "Won't you, please?"

Irene held a hand out to May, and May came forward. Instead of taking May's hand, Irene nodded to Isobel and Eleanor, because it was their turn to hold hands with May since Caroline and I had been with her on the walk. The three of them went first, with Irene falling in step between Caroline and me, taking Caroline's hand, but resting her palm on my shoulder instead.

"Are you all right, Veronika?"

"Yes, Irene."

"How was your walk?"

I began to describe where we'd gone and the distance between the waves, all to answer her original question about time. Irene brushed at the back of my smock, and I wondered if we hadn't got rid of all the sand.

"That's very good," she said, interrupting me and turning to Caroline. "And that was very good with the bird. It was just what you were supposed to do."

"Thank you, Irene."

Irene took my hand, too, then, and we were quiet the rest of the way. At the crest of the path we saw the kitchen windows with a light already on. At one point Caroline stumbled, kicking sand. Irene held tight, steadying her as if nothing had happened, and I looked to find Caroline staring at me. Then she nodded past me at a break in the dune grass, and started blinking. I almost turned to look in the same place but knew enough not to. No one stumbled the rest of the way.

• • •

After dinner we watched Robbert change the bandages on May's feet and sat outside to see the stars. May fell asleep on the steps, leaning against the rail, and Robbert carried her to bed. He came back a few minutes later and stood listening to the rest of us sing about clouds.

> *Fluffy and puffy so high in the air,*
> *We drift on the wind with nary a care.*
> *Tall as a castle and white as the snow,*
> *Where the wind takes us, that's where we go.*

Robbert said he felt like walking to the beach, and that he would see us in the morning. We waved good night and then Irene stood with her teacup, and we all went to get ready for bed. When we were on our cots with our smocks off and folded, Irene turned out the light and leaned back against the counter. She pulled out her clip and shook her head so her hair came loose around her face.

"You know that before sleep I sometimes tell you something—something to think about and wake up to. Tonight, I'm going to tell you all a story. It's a real story, something that really happened, a long time ago, that I think you ought to know. Something you can think about."

"Is tonight different?" asked Eleanor.

"Tonight is tonight," replied Irene, "and not last night."

"And not tomorrow," said Isobel. "But tomorrow we'll be able to think of the story."

"That's right. Lay back now."

Irene poured herself a cup of water from the filter. We all got settled. Irene finished her water and put the cup in the sink. I could hear the night outside. I could hear Irene breathe.

"Once there was a girl—"

I wanted to know how old the girl was and what color her hair and if she had a name, but once we lay down interruptions weren't allowed.

"—and she lived in the part of the world where people knew things. Now, everyone knows something, but in this part of the world some people knew more. Invisible things, secrets a person couldn't see without learning, without *school*. Like your school. The people who went to those schools mixed together with the people who didn't, the people who believed—well, who just believed. Sometimes that worked out but other times, and eventually most of the time, the school people had to keep themselves as hidden as the secret things they knew."

Irene stopped talking for long enough that I wondered if it was the end, but finally she kept going.

"Eventually people didn't know who knew things and who didn't, because those people were hiding, because those people who didn't learn became frightened of what they couldn't see, frightened about what was real—what was possible. And people who get frightened become angry. So the girl who knew things also knew she had to stay hidden. Because if anyone saw her, they would hurt her for the things she knew. So she left her home to find another. She sailed away. She even flew in an airplane. Just to make sure. But you can never be sure. You can never be sure. And that's what the girl learned, and she never forgot it, no matter how old she got, or how happy she was."

Irene sighed, and pushed herself up from the counter. The story was finished, even though I still had all my questions. She came to Isobel, then Caroline, then Eleanor. Her shadow passed over my face, and I felt her hand behind my ear. Irene dropped to a crouch and whispered.

"I watched you, Veronika. I saw you stand. You did so well, honey. You didn't need me at all."

I wanted to tell her it wasn't true, that I needed her forever, but by then I was already gone.

7.

It was three days until I could visit Caroline's spot in the dune grass. The days in between went almost like always, with smocks and breakfast, and walks and class and naps and more class and dinner and the porch and finally sleep. The difference was May, whether she was at breakfast or still sleeping, whether she sat with us on the porch, or whether she went walking alone to the woods. Most of all, the four of us felt May's presence from Robbert and Irene.

They would go in the other room or walk outside and close the door, but sometimes the words came without warning, unexpected even to them. Irene would give Robbert a look and he would snap, just like he'd burned his finger on a wire.

"Look, I haven't heard anything."

"But what does that *mean*?"

"Irene—it could still be the storm. It could be their receiver—"

"You're sure about ours." All four of us remembered where Robbert had been with the tools.

"I am."

"And what if it's something else?"

And that was when Irene's gaze went through the window to the classroom where May lay still asleep.

We spent that morning talking about words and how May's words didn't sound like Robbert's or Irene's, or ours. It wasn't anything we had noticed, because we'd been able to understand her perfectly well, but today Irene focused on all the variations. One example was how May didn't pronounce the *g* in words that had "ing" at the end. Another was how her letter *s* was spoken with an invisible *t* in front of it, so "sad" became "tsad." Irene explained where May's tongue was placed inside her mouth to make each sound, and showed us with her own mouth how it happened. Robbert's questions were about how our hearing turned a wrong sound into a right one. He made up sentences as if May were saying them to test our making sense.

Irene explained that ways of speaking came from different places, and that each way was like a sign announcing who a person was and what their life was mostly like and what they were most likely to believe. Isobel asked what May's way said about

May, but before Irene could answer, Eleanor asked what Irene's way said about Irene, and then Caroline asked why, if there was an agreed upon best way—the way we spoke, for example—anyone spoke a different way at all?

Irene held up her hand, which she did when we asked too many things at once. "May's life has been different. She hasn't been to the same kind of school."

"Why not?" asked Isobel.

"Because she lived on a boat. She wasn't in one place."

"Why didn't her uncle Will teach her?" asked Caroline. "Or his friend Cat?"

"I'm sure they did," Irene replied. "But they had their own work. And our school here is special. You all know more than May does. Just because she's lived in places you haven't, it doesn't mean that what she thinks about things is right."

"What does she think that isn't?" I asked, very much wanting to know.

"That depends on the thing," said Irene.

"It probably depends on the time of day," said Robbert, "and the weather, too."

Then he stood up, stuffing his notebook—because he'd been making lots of notes the entire time—into his satchel. He slung it over his shoulder and went off to his machines. We all waved good-bye, and Irene had us all do experiments where one of us left out every other word and the others tried to guess the sentence. It was easy until Irene began whispering in our ears to describe invisible things, like ideas and feelings, but even then we were able to guess because there was nothing on the island that the four of us didn't know.

As we called out our guesses I saw this was a sign about us, like the perfect sounding of our words. It was a happy thought, because right answers made Irene smile, but also because knowing this about ourselves meant that May's words—because that was where she lived—were themselves sounds of the sea, every bit as much as the crash of a wave or the cry of a gull.

More often than not May was with us, partly because she no longer needed so much sleep and partly because she finally decided to become our friend. Now that we knew about her missing school, we wanted her to answer questions, too, and get smarter. But Irene didn't ask May questions often, and when she did they weren't about the assignment. For her part, May wanted to know about Irene and about Robbert. What we first tried to tell her—how they ate and talked and moved and worked—wasn't what May wanted to hear. What she did want to hear, like where Irene and Robbert were born, and why they had left that place and come to the island, we couldn't say. Sometimes when we were alone, on walks or on the porch, May whispered questions about us as well, about why we were our size, or why some of us did different things. We always did our best to answer: about testing and control, or about being just the balanced size for our arms and legs—just like her—but our answers never made May feel better, at least not the way answers did for us.

Irene was good at not talking about what she didn't want to, of course, so when she avoided May's questions the rest of us would change the subject back to school. Even though May and Irene each kept trying to get the other to say something she wouldn't, we were all still happy to have everyone together, especially with Robbert and Irene being snappy when they thought they were alone.

"I just don't think we can," Irene had whispered, standing with Robbert in the courtyard. She had taken him a cup of tea and stood with him while we watched from the kitchen through the screen.

"What are they saying?" May had asked, but we were all trying to hear.

"It probably depends," said Robbert, talking into his teacup.

"We don't know where they'd be going next."

"No, we don't. That depends on how much they know."

"Then we can't."

"But what else—Irene, we can't pretend—"

"She's a child."

"Who *knows*. If one word—one word, Irene—"

"If we're not sure, we can't," Irene repeated, and walked

away. When she got to the kitchen we were in a line by the table, except for May.

"Everyone ready for a walk?" In the time it took to climb the steps, Irene had found her smile, the same we always saw.

That day we walked to the woods, and the next to the dock, and the one after that to the cliffs. Irene split us up like she had before, into groups of three, with her in one and May in the other. The two of us in each group changed every time, though for some reason I was never with Caroline and May together. When I was with Irene, we always talked about what we had observed. I also observed Irene: when her smile went away, or when she stared out from the cliff tops, or when her hand fell to our heads or our shoulders, patting or caressing us, which she never used to do except when we were going to sleep. In all these moments I felt, like a bone beneath skin, the sadness Irene had shown with the ruined bird.

With May it was more difficult to make observations because May never wanted to make them and, instead of making them, wanted to talk. We wanted to talk, too, but we also wanted to please Irene, so walking with May became like my visit to the dock, where I had two tasks and no rules to choose between them except my own.

Part of me—like a coconut sent rolling down a hill—had been

thinking about this problem ever since Robbert had made a point of asking me *why*. I knew that I hadn't *known* there were two tasks—the second task, my own desire, had just appeared, and somehow I had made it more important. I could be surprised by thoughts I didn't expect, because the world was more than school. May was proof enough of that—or, even more, proof that our real school was the world.

I stood in the woods with Isobel and May. Isobel and I were comparing the stiff plates of palm bark with the spiny leaves, needle-tipped and edged with tiny teeth. May wasn't interested at all. While we squatted, she glanced back at Irene.

"What is she doing?"

Irene was studying another palm trunk with Caroline and Eleanor.

"With *Robbert*," May said, interrupting me before I could say.

"Robbert isn't here," said Isobel.

May blew air through her nose. "You said there was a plane crash. Where did the plane come from? Where was it going? Who else was there?"

"Our parents," I said.

"Who *were* your parents?" asked May.

"Mothers and fathers who loved us," said Isobel. May shook her head impatiently.

"What kind of *people*? What did they swear to? Where did they live? Why were they leaving? Who has a plane? There isn't any place for a plane to land on this island. How did you get *here*?"

Isobel and I both stood. I tried to remember what Robbert and Irene had told us.

"Where they came from it rained all the time," I said. "And it was cold, and they wanted to live with the sun shining, where it was dry."

"What is 'swear to'?" asked Isobel.

May pursed her lips. "That's *everything*."

"Our parents are the kind of people who speak just like us," Isobel told May. "You speak differently."

"So do you," May replied.

"We don't."

"Well you *sound* different."

"Did Uncle Will and Cat speak like you?" asked Isobel. "Did they say '*black sand*' or '*blok tsand*'?"

May frowned at how perfectly Isobel had imitated her sounds. Then she shook her head and laughed, but it was a short laugh and she crossed both arms over her chest. She nodded at Irene.

"They don't talk like anyone I've ever met," she said.

"You don't talk like anyone we've met either," I told her.

"But I talk like more people than you," May said.

"What people?" asked Isobel.

"Everyone."

"But you don't know everyone. You lived on a boat. You didn't go to any school."

Irene called for us to join them. We each took May's hand on the way, careful not to pinch. "I didn't is right," she whispered. "And that's why I *know*."

Robbert would be waiting in the kitchen when we returned, and all during lunch he and Irene would ask us questions. At first May would answer with us, even though her answers were as if she had taken a different walk than the rest of us. Soon May stopped answering and just watched from the corner.

We were also back to taking naps. After lunch Irene would put the four of us down for a nap. There wasn't a cot for May, so she went back to the classroom; we would wave good-bye as Robbert took her down the steps. When we woke up there would be more class and then another walk, depending on how long the nap had been. May wasn't there when we woke up, but she would join us on the walk, except for the third day of our new routine.

We had gone to the dock with Robbert, but he hadn't assigned any question in particular. Instead we all just stood at the end of the path, looking out. Then he asked, "Okay now, what do you see?"

Everyone saw lots of things. We all began to answer and he

held up his hands. "No—*stop*—what do you see *now*? What do you see that you *didn't*?"

This was more of a puzzle, and so we looked around very intently. Little by little our observations drew us onto the dock itself, though we kept to the middle. I remembered about light going through water. I crouched and pressed my face to a gap between two planks, lengthwise so both eyes could see. I could see the water moving, and not just the surface. I could sense the current beneath, just from looking. The real last time we had been at the dock it was to do with numbers—how hot it was and the wind and when the tide would turn. I rose from my hands and knees, with Eleanor coming over to help me.

"Do you see more?" she asked.

"The whole water."

"And the birds." She pointed to a pair of gulls gliding above the rocks. "I looked without getting caught. I looked as hard as I could."

Robbert watched us with his hands in his pockets and a big smile on his face. Then May's head came into view, bobbing above the crest of the path. Eleanor and I both waved to her, and Robbert spun around.

"What is it?" he shouted. "Where's Irene?"

"She said I could come."

Robbert saw us watching and waved us back to work. May

caught up to where he stood and watched us, too. Her eyes were red. Even with the wind I could hear.

"Did you two have a talk?" Robbert asked.

May nodded. Her lip was shaking.

"We need your help, May. We need to know what happened. *Why*."

"I don't know why. I just woke up."

Robbert sighed. "You don't want anything bad to happen, do you?"

"Something bad already happened."

"But this is to everyone, May. Even you."

"I told her I don't know."

Robbert rubbed his mouth and stuck a finger in one ear, wiggling it. Then he clapped his hands and shouted to Isobel that she was too close to the edge.

That night I woke in the dark. At first I wasn't sure where I was, but then I saw May, kneeling by my side. She put a finger in front of her mouth. I knew this meant not to talk, but I didn't understand why. I spoke as softly as I could.

"May—"

Her hand covered my mouth and she looked over her shoulder, listening for a noise—for Irene. It was three a.m., so Irene was asleep, like she was always asleep, like everyone else. I had never been awake at three a.m. I remembered the footprint on the kitchen floor. Was being awake at night something May did all the time?

When did May learn how to wake me up?

Slowly she lifted her hand. I swung my legs over the edge of the cot, and May helped pull me to my feet. She looked into the dark of the stairs to Irene's room as we slipped through the kitchen. She opened the screen door to just before the hinge began to squeak, then motioned me through. I didn't have my smock on. What if it rained? I didn't know what was wrong— though something had to be wrong—so I decided that the best thing was to find out. May eased the door shut and I felt her standing near me, warm.

There was no moon, but the stars were bright. May took my hand and we crept down the steps, keeping on the canvas runner to muffle sound. She pulled me to the beach.

I paid attention to as many things as I could, even as May hurried me along, because this time on the island was so new. We stopped on the path and May tugged me down out of the wind, with our heads just at the level of the whistling grass. If anyone did look from the kitchen porch we wouldn't be seen.

"She told you something, didn't she?"

I didn't know who May meant, or when. May shook her head with impatience. "The other one, the one they work on more— who has dreams—"

"That's Caroline. You should know her name, May. Her hair is brown."

"Caroline. Caroline knows something, doesn't she?"

Caroline had nodded to the path, so I could tell Isobel and Eleanor, but did that include May? Would it make her mad again? I remembered Irene's story of the girl who knew things. Each time you learned something it was like a forking path that made you think something else. Would you speak or be silent? Would you finish the equation or look away? Would you follow the rules or make new ones?

"How did you know how to wake me up?" I asked.

"Sssh!" May hissed.

"Why don't you want anyone to hear?"

"Because it's a secret."

"What's a secret?"

"What they know. I heard them. They can't decide what to do with me."

"That's because you haven't been going to school. You have a lot of catching up to do, and you don't always pay attention—"

May put her hand over my mouth.

"No one can hear, May," I said through her hand.

"You don't know that. You have to whisper."

I didn't want her to be upset, so I did my best. "How did you know how—"

"I watched them—when they—when you take naps. I saw what they do. You have a spot—do you know that?"

I nodded.

"When they—when they push down—do you feel it?"

"It's the way we sleep, May. Just like you."

"I don't have a—a *button*."

"Everyone's different. But if you want to know what Caroline knows, why didn't you wake her?"

"She doesn't like me."

"Of course she likes you, May."

"I see her looking."

I couldn't say anything to that, because Caroline did look at May, but we looked at everything, which May didn't seem to understand. May was wearing her black shirt with little sleeves and her bare arms were covered with tiny bumps, because of the wind. She tucked her hands between her knees.

"I like being your friend, May. But you should be friends with everyone."

"This is stupid," May said. "You didn't tell on me, so that's why. What did she say?"

That was when I had to decide. I pointed into the grass. "There's something to look at."

"What is it?"

May pushed past me on her hands and knees, quick as a rat

through a heap of palm fronds. I came more carefully because
the dunes were sloped and it was hard to see. I reached Caroline's spot. May had gone past, rooting impatiently through the
grass.

"Back here," I called, trying to whisper.

"There's isn't anything."

"Then it must be buried."

"Bloody hell," May muttered.

"What does that mean?"

May snorted. "It means bloody hell. It means we're stupid."

"But we aren't stupid. We're finding out."

May didn't answer. There was only one spot not covered by
grass, so that's where she started digging, scooping handfuls of
sand between her legs. The hole got bigger and May spread her
legs to straddle it. The deeper ground was moist and stiff. May's
fingers knocked against something hard. She pulled back a hand,
wiped the dirt on her shorts, and stuck it in her mouth.

"Bloody hell," she said again, like she was angry.

Something lay stretched across the bottom of the hole, disap-
pearing into the dirt on either side. May scooped more sand
until we could see it all.

It was a wooden plank, covered with slick white paint, hard
and shiny like the lacquered box for Irene's hairpins. Straight
through its middle were three round holes—like a nail had been

punched again and again. I'd never seen a nail that thick, and I didn't know why anyone would put a nail through a plank like that after it had been painted.

May stared down.

"It's a wooden plank," I said. "Painted white."

All at once May began to refill the hole, shoving dirt back with both arms, then scooping clean sand on top. She pushed past me back to the courtyard.

"Let's go."

"What was it, May? May!"

"Keep your voice down!"

"You have to tell me. I'm your friend."

May spun round. "It was on purpose." Her cheeks were wet and her voice was thick. "Someone *did* it. And I'll do *them*."

She started off without another word, keeping quiet all the way to the steps. May brushed the sand off my legs and we crept inside. There wasn't a sound from Irene, or anyone. I lay down and saw May's face above me.

"Don't be afraid," I whispered.

May opened her mouth to say that she wasn't afraid, but then just nodded. She groped behind my ear but couldn't find the spot. I turned my head to make things easier, and she finally got it right.

When I woke it was Robbert's face above me, with Irene past his shoulder.

"Thank goodness," she said, and sighed.

Robbert leaned back and patted my leg. The other cots were empty. "Do you know what time it is, Veronika?"

I did know. "It's four o'clock in the afternoon."

"Can you tell us where you've been?"

I hesitated and Irene spoke more gently. "You wouldn't wake up, Veronika. We've been working very hard all day to help you."

"Why not?" I asked.

"That's the question," said Robbert. "Do you remember anything, from when you were asleep,"

"Like a dream?"

"Just like a dream," said Irene. "Did you have one?"

The last thing I remembered was May's fumbling hand. I wondered where the others were, and if May was with them, and if she had told them what we'd found.

But then I began to blink.

Irene gently turned my head so she could see my eyes. "Veronika?"

"I don't know when it was," I said, "or even if it happened, but I can think of it. Is that a dream?"

"Why don't you tell us?" asked Robbert. His hand slipped under my hair, the fingers probing softly.

"It was one of May's photographs."

"Which one?" asked Irene.

"The seventh one, with May on her boat, on the *Mary*."

"But why?" Irene shook her head and started again. "Not why did you dream—what part of the photograph feels important?"

"Zebra stripes." They both stared like they hadn't heard. "That's what Isobel called the bandages against May's skin. In the seventh photo she has a bandage on her finger, so that's one stripe, and the line of freckles beneath her eyes is another darker stripe, and then on the boat, the wood edging the deck is white, but the side of the boat under it is black, so the white is a stripe, too. Then the dark water and the bright sky are stripes, too. And the teeth in May's mouth and the white of her eyes. Except for May's green shirt almost the entire photograph is light and dark stripes pointing different directions."

"But why is that important? Why did you think about that when you should have been asleep?"

"I don't know."

"Think hard, Veronika."

I was blinking, trying to know the right words. "It was May's eyes. The pupils of May's eyes. They're like round holes. Black circles in the whites. I thought if I could look in them—all the way, if she would let me—it would explain where she had been, and it would say what had happened in the storm."

"May's eyes?" asked Irene.

"They were round hard holes."

Irene nodded. But it was only because of the buried plank that the eyes seemed that way—that was the real source of my dream, yet I couldn't ask why that would happen without telling them where I'd been. Did they know? They looked at me without speaking. I felt how hard it was to have a secret, how secrets made you feel apart and alone. Now May was on one side of a secret and Robbert and Irene were on the other.

Robbert patted my head and looked at Irene.

"Am I sick?" I asked. "Like May?"

"No, Veronika," said Irene. "We think it was a bit of sand."

"I've never had a problem with sand."

"No," said Robbert. "You haven't. So from now on you have to be extra careful, don't you?"

I nodded. Robbert and Irene led me into the kitchen. Everyone else was on the porch, waiting to come in, and when they did we all began to make an early dinner, since it didn't seem like Robbert and Irene had ever eaten lunch.

Dinner was noodles, but with a new recipe that used half the sauce and half the vegetable protein. We went to bed earlier than normal and there was no time to talk to May or for any of the others to talk to me.

As I lay on my cot, waiting for Irene, I wondered again if I should say where we'd been. She knelt next to me, her hand brushed through my hair.

"Irene?" I whispered. "Were you scared for me?"

"The important thing is that we knew just what to do. Were you scared, Veronika? Are you scared now?"

I shook my head, because I didn't know. Being scared of water made sense because it was dangerous. Could you be scared of something invisible, that you couldn't name? Irene slipped her fingers to my spot.

"Good. Sleep well, Veronika."

The next morning Irene used the same tea bag as the day before, and for lunch she made her sandwich with peanut butter. That meant we could expect the supply boat any day.

But five days later the boat still hadn't come.

8.

Since we had never actually seen the supply boat, it wasn't so much that we expected to see it now. But we kept waking from our naps to find Irene still eating peanut butter and no stack of new boxes in the kitchen, and we began to wonder why, especially when Robbert went to the cliffs with his toolbox almost every afternoon.

Our walks began to skip the dock, and as the days went on we began to skip everywhere except the woods. I thought this was because Robbert was at the aerial—so we didn't go to the cliffs. And because of my own accident with sand we didn't go to the beach. But then we began to just stay in the courtyard, which wasn't so much of a walk at all and more what Irene called focused study, which usually meant that we watched bugs.

Isobel found a black centipede and everyone went to look.

Irene asked Eleanor to list the different parts of the centipede and the rest of us to make sure she didn't skip anything. But instead of looking at the centipede, I looked at May. She wore her shirt with the flowers, the bottom button undone and the shirt-tails pulled by the breeze so I could see her stomach, soft, brown, and round in a way our stomachs weren't. The scab on her face had peeled away, leaving a pink shadow, shaped like the bones of coral. The bandages had come off her feet as well, and May no longer wore flip-flops, because she said she didn't need them.

"You can count them all together!" May snapped impatiently. "They're all the same!"

Eleanor had been listing the centipede's legs one by one, which was a lot of legs. She looked at May and cocked her head. "But they do different things."

"No they don't! They're all legs!" May raised her hands and wiggled her fingers to imitate ten of the centipede's legs in motion.

"But each leg makes a different part of the centipede move," said Caroline. "Doesn't it?"

She turned to Irene, but Irene was looking at the classroom. She realized we were waiting and spoke to me. "What do you think, Veronika?"

"I think Eleanor is right because every leg is necessary. But May is also right because every leg is by itself the same as the others."

"Very good."

"But do we count them together or not?" asked Isobel.

"You can do either," Irene replied. "The important thing is that you know there's another way. If it's the very first time you've seen something, you should count like Eleanor. But after that, you can count like May, as long as you know the difference."

"The first way is useless," muttered May.

"No, it isn't," said Isobel.

"No, it isn't," Irene echoed. May didn't say anything. "All right," Irene went on, "everyone keep looking. Don't leave the courtyard. I'll be right back."

She crossed to the classroom steps and went inside, the screen wheezing shut behind. We stood in a clump for a moment but finally nosed around in different directions. After a minute of this, I realized I was between Caroline, kicking at a tuft of grass, and May, still looking after Irene.

"We found the plank," I whispered. Caroline stood and cocked her head.

"What plank?"

"In the grass. Under the sand. The one you found."

"Found when?"

"After the storm."

Caroline began to blink. "When?"

"You found it on the beach and Robbert took it to bury. He told you not to tell. It had three holes in it."

"Bullet holes," whispered May, who was listening.

"What?" I asked. She hadn't said anything about the holes before. "What is bullet?"

May snorted and shook her head. "Bloody hell . . ."

But Caroline just stood there, eyes fluttering like moth wings at a window. "I don't remember."

"You have to remember. You told me where to look."

"Then how can I not remember?"

"Because of him," whispered May.

"Was it a dream?" Caroline asked me. "Did I forget because of that?"

"Didn't *you* have a dream?" This was Isobel. She had come near with Eleanor. "When you had trouble with sand, Veronika? Is it something *you* remember?"

"I did have a dream, but that was different."

"It's not a *dream*," said May. "I saw it, too."

"Maybe you both dreamed together," Isobel suggested.

"That's stupid," said May. "Caroline told us. She told Veronika. He did something." She pointed to the classroom. "He took her in there and he took it away. None of you know what's real. You just know what they tell you!"

Irene pushed open the screen. A lock of her hair had fallen

loose, a dark line dropped across one eye. She saw us standing together and clapped her hands.

"What is this? Back to work! I don't know what's come over you girls!"

We hurried apart to find more bugs, except for May, who stayed. Irene saw that she hadn't moved and frowned. She waved for May to come over. When May reached the porch Irene put a hand on each of May's shoulders and whispered something none of us could hear. Then the two of them went inside.

After our nap May wasn't there. Robbert woke us, which wasn't normal. Instead of going anywhere, even to the kitchen, he said we should have a talk.

"Where is Irene?" asked Eleanor.

"That's part of the talk," Robbert replied. "Irene is looking for May."

"Is May lost?" My voice was loud. "Did she fall off the cliff? Did she go in the water?"

Robbert held out his hands. "No—no, it's nothing like that. Nothing has happened to May. Nothing is going to happen to her."

"Then where is she?" I asked.

"She's . . . she's hiding."

"Why?" This was Caroline. "Why does she need to hide? Do we need to hide, too?"

"No one needs to hide," said Robbert, getting sharp. "Everyone is fine. May is upset. She's still sad, about the storm, about everything she lost. She's going to be sad for a long time, no matter how nice we are to her. She's going to be sad and angry."

"May *is* angry," said Eleanor. "More than anyone."

"And when she's angry, it isn't your fault. Or anyone's fault. And deep inside May knows that. That's part of the reason she's gone, to be by herself for a while. It's probably the best thing for everyone."

"Then where is Irene?" asked Isobel.

"Irene is trying to find her—"

"But why? If hiding is the best thing—"

"Because—to make sure—so we know where she is, just in case. Just to know that she's okay."

"Can we see if she's okay, too?"

"Not now."

"Can we see if she's okay later?"

"We'll see. Right now we have to talk."

"Talk about what?" asked Eleanor.

"About hiding?" asked Caroline.

"No. And I need everyone to listen."

We all leaned forward on our cots, because we were good at listening. Robbert scratched his nose with his thumb, which helped him decide how to say things. "I also want you to think.

We always want you to think, whatever happens. Never forget that. Even if there's no school—if no one is asking questions—if neither Irene nor I is there—"

"What about May?"

"Veronika, be *quiet*." Robbert rubbed his eyes by sticking two fingers under his glasses. "Keep your questions to yourselves. Solve them yourselves, all right? You can do that. You can. Right now you need to listen."

Making sense of what Robbert said was hard. I could imagine being without him or Irene—like when we went on separate walks—but since it was always temporary and since we talked together afterward and since whatever we did think by ourselves was always rethought depending on the others, I didn't see why that was so important. I wondered if this was a new assignment—to find May by thinking.

"Instead of talking about May," Robbert began, "I want to talk about your parents."

All four of us began to blink. No one had said anything about our parents for a very long time, except for May, who just reminded me how much I didn't know. Apparently Robbert and Irene knew more after all, though they always said they'd told us everything. And now, because we had been very good and studied hard, he had finally decided to tell us.

"The four of you are not like other girls. You're not like May.

You know that, because you've seen her, but you don't know why. May doesn't know why either. No matter what she's said to you, she doesn't know. May has no idea. She's ignorant. Don't ever forget that. Do you understand?"

We nodded.

"Good. You're all going to be smarter than she is. You're going to be smarter than anyone. And that is because of your parents. Most people have a mother and father, but you four girls had eight mothers and eight fathers. And together they all made each of you. They all made different parts, but each parent cared for each one of you just as much as the others. You are all extremely special. You're not like anyone else. But when you're made by that many parents you get made a different way—the whole *project* is different. It takes time, and it takes up space, all to make four girls. There are places where that work can happen and places where it can't. And the thing is, those places change. Because some people . . . well, they get angry at what's different, angry at what they don't understand. All right?"

I nodded, doing very well not to interrupt. We had so many things to ask.

"Good. Now, we told you there was a plane crash. There was a plane crash. And all your parents were killed. But there were two planes that day. One of them exploded and one of them didn't. The truth is that the explosion wasn't an accident. Your parents' plane exploded deliberately." Robbert stopped to scratch his nose. "People stopped it from taking off by blowing it up—angry people—ignorant people—and everyone on that plane was killed. The second plane escaped. Only Irene and I were on it, and the four of you. You were still asleep. You didn't wake until we got you here. And what you need to know—what we haven't told you—is that these angry people haven't changed. Do you understand?"

What we all understood was why Robbert was telling us now.

"Is that what happened to the *Mary*?" asked Caroline.

Robbert didn't snap at her, so Isobel leaned forward.

"Why would anyone sink the *Mary* if May only had two parents?"

"That doesn't make sense," said Eleanor.

"Is it because of the numbers in the picture?" asked Caroline.

"Does the *Mary* mean angry people came near our island?" I asked.

As soon as it was said, everyone knew my question was the most important one of all, and we waited for Robbert to reply. He nodded when he saw us waiting, and took a breath to think. This became a different kind of talking, an answer he had to make right now, almost as if Robbert were in class along with us.

"We don't think so," he said. "They would already be here. When they find what they don't like, they destroy it. Because it scares them—and you girls would scare them as much as any-thing they've ever seen."

"Why?" asked Isobel.

"Because . . . because of what they *believe*." He waved his hand to say it wasn't something he wanted to describe. "So we can't let anyone tell them. Do you understand? Not *anyone*."

"We won't," said Eleanor.

"May won't either," I said.

Robbert stared into my eyes.

"Where do you think May is now, Veronika?"

Since I already wondered if Robbert wanted us to find her, I was ready for his question. "Maybe in the dune grass, crouching down?"

"Maybe." Robbert kept up his stare. "But you don't *know*. Just like you don't really know what she'll say."

"I'm sure she wouldn't," I said. "Not if we ask her to promise."

"No, Veronika. Think. Facts. What we know most about May is that we *can't* predict what she's going to do. Because that's the difference between two parents and sixteen. You girls can do many things at once, but not things you don't decide. May can do things—she *will* do things—without any decision at all. She'll do things and then be sorry for them, after it's too late. She'll do things—*say* things—without even realizing what she's done. And *then* what?"

Robbert leaned back and crossed his arms, which meant it was time for us to think. I knew he didn't believe me about May, but I didn't know who else she could talk to on the island. The only others were the men on the supply boat—now a whole week overdue—and since we never saw them because of naps, it was just a matter of making sure May took her nap along with us. But then I thought of the aerial and Robbert's machines in the classroom and telling the supply ship when to come and what to bring. Since May lived on a boat, did she know how to contact the supply boat, too? What if she contacted the wrong boat by mistake? How many other boats were there? How many nights had May spent with the machines? She'd seen how to wake me up. How many times had she watched Robbert with his tools? Was that why Irene had gone to look for her?

"Did all of our parents love us?" asked Eleanor.

"They did," said Robbert. "Of course they did. Every bit as much as Irene and I do. And you've turned into just the girls they dreamed you'd be."

There were so many more questions—names, hair, skin, voices, smells, everything. We wanted to know as much as we could about every parent, but Robbert said it was time to go outside. We followed him down the steps. Knowing how many people had been on the plane that exploded made me think of how lonely Robbert and Irene must have been afterward. How would I feel if I was alone with only Eleanor, never to see Isobel or Caroline ever again, or Robbert or Irene, or May? I had always assumed that Robbert and Irene were the most important people to each other in the world, but now I realized I didn't know that at all. What were their lives before the plane crash—and us—had bound them together?

What was it like to live with sixteen parents? If they were as different as Robbert and Irene, did that mean that some were also more like each other, were closer than the rest? Was there someone that Irene loved more than Robbert, or even more than us? I knew they did love one another because Irene would sometimes pat Robbert's head when he said something cranky, just like she would pat ours when we said something smart. And sometimes Robbert would surprise Irene, by making tea when she hadn't had time, or ask us to sing a song as a surprise, and Irene would smile.

But they didn't hold hands with each other the way they'd taught us to, even when they weren't already carrying things like teacups or notebooks. Caroline once asked Irene why not, and Irene said, "That's because we're all grown up."

"Will we stop holding hands when we're grown up, too?"

"That will be up to you."

That was another time when Irene had patted someone's

head—that day Caroline—because she'd said something to make her smile, but now I had more of Irene's smiles to compare with one another, and I knew her smile that day was like the smiles when we found her thinking about something else.

Robbert saw we were lined up, waiting. He slung his satchel over one shoulder and told us to walk in pairs and pay attention. I took Eleanor's hand and we followed Robbert to the dock, or almost to the dock, because we stopped at the crest of the path, so we could see down all the way to the water. Robbert scuffed with his toe, shoving the red dirt into a little mound. He reached into the satchel and took out a sealed plastic tub, the kind we used to store uneaten food.

"What's that?" asked Eleanor.

"Rice." Robbert set the tub on the little mound and stepped away.

From there we followed Robbert around the island in a wandering path—to the beach, through the meadow, and to the trees, in each spot leaving a plastic tub of rice. I hoped there wouldn't be any extra dinner that night, because we wouldn't have any tubs to store it. At each spot Robbert made a point of turning a circle with his eyes, studying the landscape. When we started up the hill to the cliffs, we saw Irene walking down toward us. She waved and the four of us waved back.

"Any luck?" Robbert called.

Irene shook her head. She had a plastic jug of water slung over her shoulder.

"We've been putting out rice," called Isobel.

"We certainly have," said Robbert. He took another tub from his satchel and looked for a place to put it. "How about some rocks?"

Because we had done this on the beach with coral, we knew what he meant, and scattered to find rocks to make a pyramid so the tub of rice would be more visible.

"I've got two more left," Robbert told Irene. "I was thinking one on the cliff trail and one higher up."

"Why don't you do those by yourself?"

"Good idea. Nothing?"

Irene shook her head. Robbert huffed through his nose. By then we were piling the rocks we'd found. We stepped back so Robbert could set down the tub.

"These are for May, aren't they?" I asked.

"We don't want her to go hungry," said Irene.

"Or thirsty," said Caroline, pointing to the jug of water.

"No," said Irene. "Maybe I'll leave this here, too."

She slipped the strap off her shoulder and set it down next to the tub.

"Do we need another pyramid?" asked Isobel.

Irene shook her head, then she clapped her hands. "All right—now *I'm* hungry. Let's see what we can find for dinner."

She held out her hands for Isobel and Caroline, so once more I took Eleanor's, and we fell in step down the hill. Eleanor looked back, and then so did I, just in time to see Robbert disappear around the turn.

Irene sent us on to the kitchen, while she went into the classroom. She joined us only a few minutes later, so whatever she needed to do hadn't taken long. Once more we used a new recipe to make soup—dried vegetables, rice, and vegetable protein, but not as much of any as usual. "I've become a little fat," Irene explained, and she patted her stomach with the flat of hand, making a *whap* sound.

"Are we fat, too?" asked Eleanor. She was cutting the square of vegetable protein into strips, almost like noodles.

"Of course not," Irene replied. "You are all perfect. I remember being that big. It was a very nice size."

Isobel tipped a cup of rice into the pot. "If you keep eating less, will you be our size again?"

"That would be nice, wouldn't it? But that isn't how it works."

"If we ate things would we get big as you?" I asked.

"That isn't how it works, either," said Irene. "We're a little different, even if we look the same, or look a lot the same. And everything eats something different—like some birds eat crabs, and some other things, like palm trees or grass, eat something else entirely, like sunlight. Like energy."

She patted Eleanor's hair and scooped the strips of vegetable protein off the cutting board into the steaming water.

"What about May?" I asked.

"May needs to eat like me."

"Did you see her this morning? Do you know where she is?"

"I didn't, Veronika. I don't."

"Do you know for sure she didn't fall into the water?"

Irene waited until the soup was simmering before she gave an answer. She poured water from the filter jug into a cup.

"What do *you* think?" she asked me.

I didn't want to think, because I didn't know for sure. I wanted Irene to know for sure and tell me. I shook my head. Irene turned to the others.

"Someone must be able to think."

"I can think," I said.

"But now you don't want to, is that it?" Irene turned to the others. "Isobel, why do you think Veronika doesn't want to?"

"Because of May," said Isobel.

"Because May and Veronika are special friends," said Eleanor.

I didn't like everyone looking at me like I was different—because their looking *made* me different—but also because of Eleanor. Her words were a statement about me but held a question inside, and the question was why had I become different from her, and how that made Eleanor—and me, hearing it—both feel alone.

"I am friends with everyone," I said.

"But there are people we can't be friends with," Caroline said. "Angry people, like Robbert said."

"May is angry a lot," said Isobel.

"May isn't one of those people," I told her. "They sank her boat."

"No, she isn't," said Irene. "But May is different from all of us, isn't she?"

"May doesn't go to school," said Isobel.

"May doesn't care," said Eleanor.

"She cares about some things," said Caroline, "but not the same ones. She knows how to sit on the edge of a cliff or walk in the water, but not how to read or use numbers."

Suddenly I understood it. Of course May hadn't fallen. My being frightened for her was just like our not paying any attention to the peak.

"There are places we wouldn't know," I said. "Small places where you have to climb or squat or jump. That's why you don't think she fell."

Irene stirred the soup. "What do we do when we want to know something?"

Eleanor answered before anyone else, though all of us knew. "To know why a bird flies you have to know what it wants from flying—if it wants to catch bugs in the air or crabs on the rocks. So to know where May went, we have to know what she wants from going."

"To be alone," said Caroline.

"Because she's still sad," said Isobel. "But how long does being sad last?"

I turned to Irene. "Are you still sad about our parents?"

Irene took a moment to answer. "Sadness can last your whole life, Veronika. But it doesn't mean you can't also be happy, too. We'll give May as much time as we can—and hopefully that's all the time she needs." Irene tapped the spoon on the rim of the cooking pot and then set it to the side. She put the lid on the pot and lowered the flame to a flickering blue ring. "There. We'll wait for Robbert and eat when he gets here."

Over dinner no one mentioned May at all. Instead we were finally able to ask more questions about our talk with Robbert, which was better because now Irene could answer, too. But the most interesting part wasn't even an answer to what we asked, but Irene talking instead about life in a place full of rain: what extra clothes she had to wear, how the air was damp, about rust and mold, about hats made of plastic, umbrellas, whole villages on stilts, not seeing the sun for weeks at a time—almost the exact opposite as our island—and about how many places where people lived had turned into islands, and how many older islands had disappeared. By the end of her story all four of us were quiet from how dangerous it must have been. When Eleanor said this out loud, Robbert leaned close to her, so we could see her eyes reflected in his glasses.

"That's exactly right, Eleanor. And that's why we had to leave."

As I folded my smock for sleep I wondered if May would come wake me like before. I wondered what she thought in her hiding place, and if she thought of us—if she knew how much we thought about her or if she only cared about the rest of her life, the part that had disappeared in the storm.

But when I woke it was the next morning, with Irene's hand on my shoulder.

"Are you with us, Veronika?"

"I am, Irene," I said. "Just like normal."

"Good girl. Get dressed now."

In the brightness of morning Irene's world of rain seemed very hard to believe. Our walk with Irene was an exact repetition of our walk the day before with Robbert, where he'd laid out the plastic tubs of rice. One by one we visited the tubs, from the dock to the beach, to the meadow, and finally up the hill.

The tubs were just where we'd left them, with the rice inside. Irene picked each one up and put it in her own satchel. But when we got to the spot on the cliff path—of the last tub we'd actually set down, since Robbert had done the final two farther up—the tub was gone, along with the jug of water.

Irene had us make sure it hadn't been taken by an animal—which really meant by one of the rats that lived in the palm grove—so we searched the tall grass around the path in every direction. No one found either the tub or the jug.

"All right, then," said Irene, and we kept walking up.

Robbert must have told her where he'd put the other tubs, because twice Irene had us wait while she went forward, first stepping closer than any of us would have liked to the edge of the cliff, and at a second spot climbing up the rocky peak in the direction of the aerial. Neither place had a plastic tub. We shouted out for her to be careful, especially on the peak when she went up on her toes to peer around, and her toes were perched on very small spaces in the rock. Finally she came back down. She brushed off her hands and told us not to worry. Then Irene cupped both hands around her mouth and aimed her voice up so it would carry.

"There's food waiting whenever you want, May! Don't be afraid!"

Then she took two of the other tubs of rice from her satchel and set them on the path, waving us to be still when we began to look for rocks to build a pyramid.

It took us longer to walk back, since—because of how worried we'd been—all five of us held hands in a line. The path wasn't always as wide as we needed and so sometimes one or even two of us had to push through the tall grass. By the time we reached the woods Irene had us back in groups of two and three.

"What is May afraid of?" asked Eleanor.

Before Irene could ask us what *we* thought May was afraid of, I said, "The angry people can't be why she's hiding now, because they aren't here. She must be afraid of something that *is* on the island."

At once we began to think of possibilities. Birds? Crabs? Rats? Trees? Machines?

Isobel looked up at Irene. "Is she afraid of *you*?"

"She doesn't need to be," said Irene.

"You saved her life," said Eleanor.

"She knows that," said Irene. "She's worried about something else, I think."

We waited for Irene to say more, but she only sighed. When we reached the courtyard she told us to wait while she went into the classroom. Even from where we stood we could hear the clicking of switches and Irene's voice.

"She is trying to call the supply boat," said Caroline.

"The boat is so late," said Isobel. "Did they lose their clock?"

"Maybe they lost their receiver," said Eleanor.

We heard Irene moving in the classroom, and then more switches.

"Why would May be frightened of Irene and Robbert?" asked Eleanor.

"What happened to *make* her frightened?" said Caroline. "She wasn't before."

"Maybe May made a mistake," said Isobel. "If she isn't smart."

"She isn't stupid," I said, "just different."

"She calls us stupid very often," said Isobel. "*That* is stupid."

When May had first arrived, Robbert and Irene had kept her away from us, and us away from her. We knew now May wasn't one of the people who had caused the explosion, but had they known that when she arrived? Robbert had said the four of us would scare these people more than anything. I remembered how May had first seen my face and screamed.

"They wanted to send her away," I said. "On the supply ship. But now they can't, because she's seen us. They think she'll tell people, and those people will get frightened and angry and then they'll come."

"She *would* tell people," said Isobel. "Even if she promised not to. She would get angry or scared and just spit it out."

"They'll blow us up like the plane," said Eleanor.

"We'll have to hide," said Caroline.

"We can't let May go anywhere," said Isobel.

They were right, but I shook my head. "Then why is May hiding? She won't be sent away. What does she think Robbert and Irene will do?"

We looked up at the wheeze of the screen. Irene came to the top of the stair. In her hands was a folded bundle of white canvas, cut from May's sail.

"It's time to test another idea," she called, and lifted the canvas. "Caroline's."

"A rain trap!" said Caroline.

"And just in time," said Irene. "Because there's going to be another storm."

9.

There was a time of the year when storms came more often, but two so close together was unusual. Irene called out for Robbert. When he called back, everyone had to search to find where the sound was coming from.

"Under here!" he called again, and we saw him on his hands and knees behind the classroom steps. He made a big grunting sound and a large blue plastic barrel appeared. Robbert shoved the barrel into the courtyard—yelling for us to get out of the way—and then scrambled up in front of the barrel to stop its roll.

Everyone spent the rest of the day setting up Caroline's rain trap. First the barrel was cleaned with an orange powder that Robbert mixed with water, changing it to a bright gel he rubbed · over the inside of the barrel. We thought he would then have to waste water to rinse it off, but he said that we could just filter any rainwater that the barrel caught—which we had to do anyway, because of the sky—and it would strain out the orange chemicals. After this everyone helped to hang the canvas on the slanted edge of the kitchen roof, which meant Robbert and Irene getting on the roof and all four of us holding the canvas as best we could down below. The roof made all kinds of creaking noises when they walked and both their faces got red while they worked, from the sun and the effort. Eventually they came down and we attached the ends of the canvas, which had been tied into a tube with nylon rope, to the barrel. Irene cut a new plastic lid for the barrel. It had a hole for the canvas tube but was otherwise tight so the water wouldn't evaporate (because that was the reason to make a rain trap).

They went back on the roof to make sure of all the nails and ties. Irene reached toward Robbert and tapped twice with her hammer. He looked up, but she only nodded past him. I thought this was just like Caroline telling me where the plank had been buried, so even when Robbert didn't turn to look—maybe he didn't understand her signal—I did. I couldn't see anything. Then I realized that Irene could see farther from the roof than I could from the ground. And because I was watching I saw that Robbert did look a minute later, even though he still didn't say anything.

I looked again and saw a dark shape in the grass that hadn't been there before and I guessed it was May, the black of her hair just visible as she watched what we were doing. I wanted to wave, but didn't, because neither Irene nor Robbert had done anything to let May know she'd been seen. Usually we all liked to be seen—because we liked being together—but Robbert and Irene wanted to look at May without her running away, even if she still planned to leave again after her peeking. But seeing May in the grass meant she hadn't fallen off the cliff or into the ocean, and meant she'd walked by the new tubs of rice—that she'd at least had a cold breakfast instead of nothing at all.

Worrying about May's breakfast only made me worry more about the storm, because she didn't know one was coming. I knew how dangerous it was to be caught outside, and I didn't understand why Irene and Robbert hadn't shouted *that* to her, to let her know. Of course in school they let us discover things for ourselves, so I supposed they were content to wait for the clouds to form, or even for the rain to start falling—so the decision to come back inside was one May made without anyone giving her the answer. But what if, once the rain started, May couldn't come back even if she wanted? What if the rocks were too slippery? What if she got too wet? What if the wind blew her over? What if she fell and no one heard her call for help?

I began to walk up the hill.

"Where are you going?" called Isobel.

"May doesn't know about the storm."

The others didn't know what to do. I wouldn't have known, either—whether to follow or to call out to Irene and Robbert or whether to keep quiet. By the time I'd reached the path, they'd all seen May, too. Behind me the hammering had stopped, but Robbert and Irene didn't call out. As I came near, what had been a shadow became a face, with two bright eyes. This time I waved. May didn't wave back, but she didn't run, either. Since she was faster, maybe she thought she could run whenever she liked.

May rose halfway, hunched like she was ready, so I stopped.

"How are you feeling, May?"

May looked past me and I glanced back. Caroline, Eleanor, and Isobel had followed, but just to the foot of the meadow path. Robbert and Irene watched from the roof.

"Everyone is worried, May. We thought you might have been hurt."

May shrugged, as if to say she wasn't hurt, and didn't care about our worry, either.

"Can I come closer?" I asked. "I need to tell you something. If you get scared, you can always push me over again."

"I said I was sorry." May didn't say anything else, so I came nearer.

"Did you enjoy the rice?"

"What are they doing?"

"Making a rain trap."

"Why?"

"To catch water."

"Why *now*?"

"Because there's going to be another storm."

"When?"

"Soon. You should come inside with us. It isn't safe where you are."

"You don't know where I am. No one does."

"But inside it will be warm. We'll make soup and hot tea."

May shrugged.

"You'll be cold." I took another step and May drifted backward.

"What is wrong?" I asked. "What happened?"

"It's them." She meant Robbert and Irene. "They're going to hand me over."

"They won't," I said.

"They will. I heard them. You don't know what would happen."

"What would happen, May?"

"They know. Everyone knows. Will had seen it. That's why we were so careful. You have to be careful. You can't just meet people."

Her words were like islands, just the visible tips of mountains underneath.

"But I've thought about it, May. They can't send you away. You've seen us."

May glared downhill. "Then that's even worse."

I could see her chin shake, how ready she was to run. But to where, and for how long?

"Come with me, May. Let's take a walk, just us."

I held out my hand. May didn't say anything, but when I took another step she didn't run. I kept going until she was near enough to take my hand, even though she didn't. But that was fine. I started to walk up the hill. May walked with me, and neither of us looked back.

While I was worried I would say the wrong thing and May might really push me down—and not on soft sand but on hard rocks or even near the cliff—I had other thoughts that kept me walking.

"Do you think about your uncle Will and Cat?"

May's eyes went darker. "Why?"

"Because I think we feel the same."

"No we don't. You *can't* feel like I do."

But I shook my head and explained what Robbert had told us, about the two planes and the explosion and our parents and the people who would be very frightened and angry if they found us. "Just like you were frightened. You saw me and you screamed."

"You can't blame me for that. Anyone would have." May's eyes focused on her feet as we walked, but she also peeked over, like she was trying to see me for the first time all over again. I stopped walking and let her look.

"I'm your friend. I'm a girl like you."

May glanced back down the hill. The other three were where they'd been, still watching. I waved to them, and they waved back.

"Why do you do that?" May asked. *"Wave."*

"Irene says that saying hello is a nice way to make sure everyone is okay. Waving says 'I see you'—and when someone sees you, it tells you where you are."

"I know where I am."

"But where is that, May? Where is that without anyone to help you?"

She looked like she wanted to push me.

"I heard them!" she shouted. "Of course she's going to tell! Of course they'll come! We can't take the chance!"

May made a croaking sound in her throat and spat, stabbing her head forward to send the spit as far as possible. I had almost never seen anyone spit, and didn't know that it could be another kind of speaking, angry and hard.

"They were worried, May, because of the explosion that happened with our parents. And because of the plank with three holes."

"'We can't take the chance!'" May shouted, and swatted at the grass with her feet. "What do you think that *means*?"

I braced myself to be kicked like the grass, but May didn't come near me. She stumbled farther up the hill and angrily swung her arm as if it could push us all away.

"But the boat hasn't come, May." It was important for her to know. "That's why we need the rain trap. Because we don't know when there will be more supplies. There may never be a boat again."

"It doesn't matter!" called May, retreating farther.

"But what about the storm? May! You won't be safe!"

May broke into a run. I tried to follow, but I moved too slowly. I had only gone a few yards before she was lost between the trees. She hadn't understood me at all. I needed to explain how she was wrong.

I turned to something touching my arm. It was Robbert. I hadn't heard him. Had May?

"Let her go, Veronika. We have to get back."

"But she might get hurt."

"May will be fine. She knows she can come back any time. She knows you're her friend."

"She thinks you and Irene want to put her on the boat."

"Is that what she said?"

"Or even worse."

He frowned at me. "What do you mean?"

I shook my head. "I don't know, but bad."

Robbert sighed. "Veronika, you know we only want to help her, don't you?" I nodded. He gently turned me around and started us both back down the path. "You *know* that. And you can tell her so when you next speak. But now we have to go home."

"But May—"

"Look at the sky, Veronika."

I looked. The clouds beyond the beach had become a high dark wall, advancing straight toward the island. Irene and the others were already indoors.

"Quick as you can, now," said Robbert. The wind had risen, a chilled hiss cutting through the palms.

I went as fast as I could, though downhill is harder than going up. Robbert put a hand on my shoulder. The dark clouds came quickly and the light began to dim.

"Did you finish the rain trap?"

"We did. Let's hope it holds together."

I stopped at a sudden, unexpected impact. The center of my smock was darkened by a blotch of wet cotton. A raindrop. I looked up and another spattered on my face. At once Robbert was towering over me, his body shielding mine as he tore at his white coat.

"Don't move, Veronika. Don't worry. Tuck in your arms."

I pulled both arms tight to my sides. Robbert draped his coat over my head and torso. I stood for a moment in soft darkness, and then felt a hand behind my knees and another across my back. The raindrops probed against the coat, isolated taps growing into a ragged, continuous volley. Robbert grunted with the effort of lifting me, and I shook with the heavy lurch of his steps. I felt the thud of his feet on the grass and then the harder surface of the stairs. The rain slapped on the porch. The wet coat clung to my body. The screen door wheezed and then we were inside, Irene helping to set me down and both of them wiping me with warm towels and making sure I was fine.

The others were on their cots, asleep. Outside the rainfall grew to a roar. It had happened so fast. I hoped May had reached her hiding place, and I hoped it kept her dry.

Every few weeks—the exact time depended on what we'd been doing, especially how much time we'd spent near the beach— Irene and Robbert would talk to each of us alone, asking simple questions and making us do all sorts of simple things, like moving our arms in different directions, picking up objects of different weight, making different sounds, and that was just the start. This was called "basic diagnostics." On the shelf in the classroom were four blue binders, one for each of us, where the details of every basic diagnostic had been noted down, all the way back to our beginning.

After they made sure I was dry, Irene asked me diagnostic questions, and when I was able to answer they had me walk across the room and move my arms and legs and lift things and read small type and identify sounds they made behind my back. When I did all of it, just like always, Robbert let out a big sigh and sank onto a chair. He ran his fingers through his hair and asked Irene if she wanted any tea, which was also his way of asking Irene if she would make it. I offered to make it instead, but Irene was already filling the kettle from the filter. She set the pot on the cooker and lit the blue gas ring.

Before she sat in her own chair, Irene turned out the kitchen light. This only left the glow from the gas ring, which gave a faint halo to each of their heads. I looked at my bare arms and saw them both reflect pale blue. Outside, the rain fell hard as before, and the wind pressed tight against the glass.

"Primitive man around the fire," said Robbert.

"Stop it," said Irene.

"Irene likes to listen to sounds in the dark," I said.

Robbert nodded. "I know."

I wondered when they would put me to bed with the others. I didn't want them to. The water began to hiss inside the kettle.

"What did you say to May?" Irene asked me, but at the very same time I had a question of my own.

"What is primitive?"

Our words overlapped, but since Irene's questions were always important I began to tell them everything I had said to May and what May had said back. I wasn't sure how they would react to the part where May got so angry—about overhearing Robbert and Irene—but since I didn't understand that either, I hoped they would explain it. I also wasn't sure about my telling May about the explosion, but again it seemed like she needed to know how we shared losing parents—that being the same was the best way for her to trust me.

"It's good to know she isn't hurt," said Irene, after I finished.

"But will she be hurt in the storm?" I asked.

"I don't know, Veronika. We don't know where she is. She must have found some place. I hope it's dry."

I looked up. Even though Irene's bedroom was directly above us, I could still hear rain pounding on the roof. "What place could be dry?"

"Maybe she found a cave," said Robbert.

"Are there caves?" I asked.

"There might be," Robbert's pale fingers scratched in his hair. "On the cliffs. A person would have to climb."

"How could anyone even find them to begin with?"

Robbert smiled. "How do you think, Veronika?"

"By going right to the edge and looking down? Even though that's too dangerous?"

"How else?" asked Irene.

She leaned forward to watch me thinking, and I knew they both already had the answer—that they'd known about the caves before May had ever arrived. Now it was a problem for me, to imagine a part of the island that had always been there but somehow lay beyond our consideration. I thought of the cliffs, and where May had stood, farther out, looking down.

"By the birds."

"What about them?" asked Irene.

"The patterns where they fly. From the cliff wall, when they go out of sight. The angles don't make sense unless there are places down below to stop and then start off again."

"But why is that a cave?" asked Robbert. "Why not just an outcropping of rock?"

"Because of their speed, and the angles. They have to be going farther in."

Robbert looked at Irene and smiled.

"That's very good, Veronika," she said.

I was glad to see them smile, and also to know that May did have a cave after all, even if she had to share it with birds.

The kettle began to whistle.

"O let me do it," said Robbert, waving for Irene to stay.

"I've set out the green. Only half a scoop."

Robbert tapped the loose tea from the scoop until he had the right amount, tipped it into the pot, then poured the water in after. I knew he was supposed to warm the pot with water first, and Irene knew I knew because she saw me looking. She shrugged and leaned back again. With the gas turned off, the only glow came from the machines on the counters and shelves, colored pinpricks. But these were faint, and Irene's face lay in shadow.

"Is it time for you to sleep?"

"Do I need to?"

"You've had a very big day. Escaping the storm. Were you frightened?"

"It happened so quickly, and you both were there. Are storms always so fast?"

"Not all of them. Listen to it. What do you hear?"

What I heard first was Robbert getting the teacups, so I turned to face out the window.

"It's like a finger of the sky," whispered Irene, "dragging across the world."

"The sky does not have fingers," I said.

Irene laughed. Robbert set a steaming teacup near her hand.

"I hope the trap holds up," he said.

"I wish that girl were indoors."

Now it was Robbert who shrugged. He sat with his cup. Irene didn't say anything more until finally Robbert said, "I don't want anything to happen to her, either."

"She's just a child."

"I know it. Look, I'm going to drink my tea, and then I'm going to the classroom and make sure of the windows. You should double-check upstairs."

"I will. And then what?"

"I don't know, Irene. Except this one should say good night."

"This one" meant me. "Can I wait until you've finished your tea?"

"Of course," said Irene.

I kept my face to the window. I tried to imagine the black sea and a girl struggling in its heaving waves, her body shuddering with cold.

Irene picked up her tea. I heard her blow across the cup to cool it.

We woke up together. The storm had passed and the sky was back to blue, so bright and rich it bled straight into the sea at the horizon, a giant blue bowl.

The four of us stood with Irene on the beach path, looking out. Robbert was in the classroom, testing if everything still worked. They had been up for hours, if they had slept at all, checking for damage.

When we were putting on our smocks I asked if they had seen May in the night, or any time that morning. Irene said they hadn't, but that she had walked to the cliff and called for May and left more food where she could find it.

"Are you sure she's all right?" I asked.

"I don't know, Veronika. It was a very powerful storm. But the birds survive, and she's hiding where they do, so I hope we'll see her soon. She can't be comfortable."

I told the others everything while we got dressed and went outside. We wanted to walk to the cliff, but Irene said we weren't skipping class. We knew perfectly well that class after a storm was always studying what had changed.

Three large palm leaves had blown into the courtyard, and we helped Irene put them in a pile. The day was very hot, without much wind, as if the storm had used it up. I knew there was no barrel of wind that could run out, but thinking like that was a way to imitate Irene, who sometimes described things differently from what they actually were, like saying the sky had fingers. When we were younger we would always ask why—if she said "that took forever" or "hot enough to fry an egg"—because we knew how long it had really taken and that there were nests in the trees where no eggs were being fried. But we sometimes made exaggerated points of our own, to be like her, even though she told us not to try.

Irene wiped the sweat off her neck with a kerchief, folded it over, and then stuck it into the pocket of her dress. She wasn't wearing her white coat, only an old dress without sleeves that came to her knees. Whenever I saw Irene's bare arms I thought of how strong they were and how far she could reach. Her skin was a different color than May's, more reddish from being burnt by the sun, though the parts under her arms weren't burnt. They were almost as pale as Robbert, who almost always wore his white coat, no matter how hot it was. The paleness under Irene's arms made me think of the bottom of May's feet and the palms of her hands, which were lighter, too. I didn't know if that was because of the sun—I didn't think anyone got much sun on the bottoms of their feet, but May's hands were in the sunlight all the time. The four of us didn't change color at all, even if we went outside without our smocks.

Irene shaded her eyes with both hands and studied the water. We were looking at the beach. Fresh footprints went off from where we stood in either direction.

"Have you already been here?"

She looked down at me. "We had a quick look."

"Maybe we'll find something you didn't," said Caroline.

"Because you're good at finding?" asked Irene.

"That's our job," said Eleanor.

We walked together, all five in one direction—toward where

I'd found May—keeping on past where Irene's footprints stopped, until we reached the rocks. These were the same black rocks that made the cliffs, only here they were low, rising from the sand to break up the beach, like they stuck out of the water and broke up the waves. The ground on the island rose here, so while it wasn't yet the cliffs, it was where they began. I tried to see May's cave, but the island kept curving as the ground rose. The actual cliffs were too far away, beyond a spur of rock.

What we did see, however, was what the storm had thrown onto the rocks.

"More planks." I pointed to a tangle of broken white boards, like the one Robbert had buried only longer. Since I had told the others, and since we had all talked about the *Mary* being sunk on purpose, I decided I could say "more" instead of simply "planks"—and Irene didn't correct me.

"Are they from the *Mary*?" asked Eleanor.

"Are they from the supply boat?" asked Caroline.

Irene shook her head. "The supply boat is mostly steel."

"How does steel float?" Isobel said, but then nodded, blinking. "Displacement. Could anything float with displacement? Could we?"

"If we were shaped like boats," said Eleanor.

"Just being in water is dangerous," said Caroline. "Not only sinking."

"Is anyone shaped like a boat?" Isobel asked Irene.

"I'm afraid not." Irene turned back to the debris, and we all looked with her.

"We should tell May," I said. "If they're from her boat."

"Wouldn't anything from the *Mary* have drifted away by now?" asked Caroline. "It's been weeks."

"Work out the current," said Irene.

"It depends on the storm," I said, but then I nodded to Caroline. "Probably not."

"Then whose boat could it be?" asked Eleanor. No one had an answer.

"Do you see anything else?" Irene asked.

We looked from where we were, because no one felt confident climbing out on the rocks, especially because the rocks were full of little pools. If we had seen something special Irene could have collected it, but we didn't: only knots of nylon rope, chunks of packing foam, and strips of plastic that could have once been anything.

We returned down the beach, each of us trying to walk in our original footsteps. This was one of Robbert's tests for balance, and even after we got it right we all kept doing it. We passed the beach path and continued in the other direction with Robbert's and Irene's footsteps ahead of us.

We just found more junk. Most was what Irene called natural

junk, like coconuts or driftwood or jellyfish or shells or kelp. Irene said this was how palm trees got from one island to another. With jellyfish it was different, because they were all dead. Eleanor once compared the dead jellyfish to things on land that couldn't live in the water, wondering if there were jellyfish swimming past dead sunken birds and people, wondering where they were from. It had made Robbert laugh. He patted Eleanor's head and made an entry in his notebook.

This junk was the same: coconuts and wood and kelp and jellyfish, and also regular fish as well, caught in a wave and flung up to die. Mixed in were more of what we'd seen on the rocks, except not planks, just plastic, packing foam, bottles, nylon rope.

It was disappointing, but then we came to where the back and forth tracks from Robbert and Irene stopped at the same place, where there had also been some digging.

They had reached this spot, dug something up, and then come home.

We all turned to Irene. If Irene really hadn't wanted us to know about what they'd found, she would have stopped the walk halfway.

"What did you find?" asked Caroline.

"Did you bring it back?" Eleanor tugged Irene's hand. "What was it?"

"Should we guess?" asked Isobel.

"Was it something useful?" asked Eleanor.

"Was it another plank with holes?" I asked.

But Irene wasn't listening. She stared over the water. She went up on her toes and shaded her eyes with both hands.

"Irene?" I asked.

"What do you see?" Irene asked. She extended her arm. "What do you see *there*."

We all looked. A gleaming fleck against the darker waves, spray breaking across it like a rock, except the fleck heaved up and down, in motion.

After all this time, it was a boat.

10.

We had never actually seen the supply boat, so as much as Irene hurried us back, we kept craning our heads to catch another glimpse. We talked aloud to each other, describing the color, the size, and making guesses about displacement, wind shear, speed. At the courtyard Irene called for Robbert, then waved us impatiently to the kitchen. Robbert came out, and we all shouted that the supply boat had finally come. Irene wheeled and told us to get going. Robbert ran back into the classroom.

Since we'd seen the boat from a distance, we hoped to see it up close, too, and meet the men who sailed it, because finally it had come when we were awake and ready. Irene just shook her head.

"No. Everyone on their cots."

"But, Irene—"

"No."

"But, Irene—"

"*No!* Keep your smocks on—there isn't time."

We were very disappointed. Robbert called from the yard. "I'm going ahead!"

"Be right there!" Irene called back. Robbert's footfalls went thudding off. Irene knelt next to Isobel.

"We could help," Isobel said.

"I know you could," said Irene. "That isn't why you have to stay."

"Why, then?" asked Eleanor.

"Sleep tight, Isobel." Irene touched the spot behind Isobel's ear and shifted to Eleanor. "It's because we don't know everything that's happened. Next time, if things are fine, I promise you'll see more."

"Everything that's happened where?" asked Eleanor. "Do you mean with May?"

"Sleep tight, Eleanor." Eleanor fell asleep, and Irene swiveled to Caroline. Caroline turned from Irene's hand.

"Don't."

"Don't what?" asked Irene.

"Don't go," said Caroline.

"Why not?" Irene's hand curved gently around Caroline's neck. "What's wrong?"

"I don't know. I'm trying to know, but I can't."

Irene frowned. "What makes you say that? Was it a dream?"

Caroline nodded. Irene glanced at the door, then back to Caroline. "Is it the boat?"

"I don't know."

"Is it the men?"

"I don't know. I'm sorry."

"It's not your fault, Caroline. You're doing very well. We'll talk it through when I get back." Irene's finger found her spot.

"Don't," whispered Caroline.

"We'll talk later, I promise."

Irene pressed the button and Caroline settled, fluttering eyes gone still. Irene reached for me.

"What did she know?" I asked.

"It was just a dream, Veronika."

"Sometimes her dreams come true."

Irene looked at me. "Why do you say that?"

"Caroline had a dream about hiding."

Irene sighed and shook her head, as if she'd been thinking I'd say something else. "I know she did. But no one has to hide."

"May is hiding."

"But she doesn't have to. That's different—and it's not what Caroline dreamed. Sleep tight. I'll be back before you know it."

I felt her hand behind my ear.

"I love you, Irene."

Her finger found the spot but didn't press. Irene bit her lip.

"Why did you say that?"

"Because I do."

"But why? What does that mean? Veronika—why do you say *love*?

"Because." I felt like I was on the dock, so alone. I felt like I was on my face in the sand, struggling. "Isn't that the right word?"

"Word for what, honey? Why do you say it now?"

I shook my head. I didn't know. Irene smiled and sighed at the same time.

"I love you, too, Veronika. Don't you forget it."

I felt her lips on my forehead, soft and warm, and then the click.

There are different ways to understand time, different units to count. We knew minutes and hours and seconds without even thinking—as just part of waking up—but as we learned more about the world, our vocabulary for time expanded, too. It could be small things like meals—how long one took to make or eat— or how often the water filter had to be refilled, or how often Irene or Robbert went to the chemical toilet. It could be larger forces that touched the entire island, like tides or moons or seasons or birds laying eggs or grass flowering. We named these as increments, regular and repeated, each one a new-sized gear whose interlocking teeth made up the schedule of our world.

More complicated were the increments that floated alone: flights of birds, or the time it took us to reach the beach compared to Robbert, or to Irene, or how many whacks with the machete it took to open a coconut, depending on the person and also the coconut. As we grew capable of noticing all these measurements we couldn't *not* notice them, and so every different increment joined with hundreds, and then thousands, of others. And because we didn't forget things, our understanding kept everything ready to connect.

May, of course, presented entirely new measurements, and while we had figured out some of them—how wide she stepped, how long she took to eat—a lot still remained uncertain because of how sick she'd been when she arrived. We knew May was faster than us, but not how much, mainly because her feet had been hurt. Was she faster than Robbert or Irene? We didn't know, but we were watching.

So when I woke to find May kneeling next to me, out of breath, her body moist with sweat, I didn't know how long it had taken her to reach the kitchen from her hiding place on the cliffs. I knew that it had been twenty minutes since Irene had left us, and that it took Robbert half an hour to walk down from the cliffs. It seemed probable that May had come down in a hurry at almost the same time the five of us had seen the boat.

"Get up!" she hissed. "Get up! We have to go!"

"What's wrong?"

May pulled with both hands to heave me up, though I was too heavy. I caught myself before I fell, and moved my legs off one at a time so I could stand.

"Where are Irene and Robbert?" she asked.

"They went to meet the supply boat," I said. "But now you're here, maybe we can all get a peek."

"Bloody hell! They could be here any minute!" May flung herself toward Isobel's cot and began groping behind her ear.

"May, it's all right—Robbert and Irene won't make you do anything you don't want."

"It's not Irene and Robbert!"

"May, you have to be gentle—"

"Wake 'em up!" she cried. "Wake 'em up! We have to go!"

"May—"

"We don't have time!"

She found Isobel's spot, and Isobel blinked awake. May moved to Eleanor. "Get her up!" she called to me, meaning Isobel.

"What's happening?" asked Isobel.

"I don't know," I said. "May says something is wrong. The supply boat—"

"That's no supply boat!" snarled May as Eleanor stirred to wakefulness.

"But Irene saw it," said Isobel. "Didn't she recognize it?"

May shook her head. "Then she wasn't paying attention!"

"Tell us why, May." I reached for her arm, but she pushed me away and hurried to Caroline. "May, what did you see?"

When we had a lot of things to think at once, our eyes blinked. With May it seemed like too many words came into her mouth from different directions. Her jaw worked and the thoughts came out in bits.

"Everyone knows—Will told me. You can tell! They have a flag!" May shut her eyes and waved her hands. "They don't even care—because they don't care if you know—they're coming anyway! And there's nothing anyone can ever do!"

She thrust her fingers under Caroline's head, searching for the spot.

"You have to be gentle!" cried Isobel.

May ignored her. She pressed the spot, and Caroline shifted on her cot. "We have to go! We have to hide!"

"But where are Irene and Robbert?" asked Eleanor.

"They must still be at the dock," I said.

"Do they know about the flag?" said Eleanor.

"May said everyone knows," said Isobel.

"We don't," said Eleanor. "May, *who* is in the boat? Who is coming?"

May groaned aloud, looking down at Caroline. "Why won't she get up?"

Caroline's eyes flickered.

"She's had a dream," said Eleanor.

"What?"

"When Caroline dreams, she wakes up slowly," said Isobel.

"There isn't *time!*" cried May. Her eyes had filled with tears.

A sound we'd never heard chopped through the air, echoing across the island. A flat, loud, rattling crack, like a chain yanked fast through an iron loop. It came from the dock.

"O no," whispered May. "O no."

I reached for Caroline's arm, like Irene did. "Caroline, wake up!"

Caroline rolled her head toward me, still blinking.

"The notebook," she said.

"May says we have to go."

"Take Robbert's notebook."

We got Caroline to sit. Isobel stood at the door, holding the screen open and listening.

"What was that sound?" she asked.

Caroline's head tilted to one side. One eye blinked faster than the other. "I remembered. They want us to take the notebook."

"It isn't here," said Eleanor, looking around her.

"Then it's in the classroom," said Isobel.

"We have to go," said May, tugging Caroline toward the door.

"It's important," insisted Caroline.

"I'll get it." I let Isobel take my place with Caroline and went out first.

"You can't!" hissed May behind me.

"Go ahead," I whispered back. "I'll catch up!"

I glanced once at the dock path, then crossed the courtyard as fast as I could.

I hadn't been inside the classroom since we'd crept in to look at May. The bedsheets were balled into a pile, as if Robbert meant to wash them but hadn't made time. The rest of the classroom looked just as disorganized, with things in stacks and boxes pulled out and left open. The boxes were for supplies, so it seemed Robbert had opened them to find out what they needed from the supply boat. I realized the pallet cart hadn't been under the classroom porch. Robbert must have taken it to the dock, so they could carry back everything the boat delivered.

I didn't understand what made Caroline dream, but Irene and Robbert always considered it important. If she thought we needed Robbert's notebook, it was because some inside part of her had been given a question—or realized the question should be asked—and this was the answer she had found.

Because of the boxes and the piles, I didn't see the notebook right away—or, I didn't *not* see it, because it took me longer than normal to see it wasn't anywhere. I searched the desk and looked underneath piles, all the time knowing I had to move fast. The notebook usually lived on the desk or in Robbert's satchel. I didn't see his satchel anywhere in the classroom. Did he have it with him?

The back room was full of machines stacked in metal shelves, with whirring fans to keep them cool. I saw the window where I had peeked in. The notebook wasn't there, either.

The kitchen had an upper floor where Irene slept, reached by a set of narrow stairs. Because the top of the classroom was filled with batteries connected to the roof panels, there wasn't enough room for a proper bed—which was why Robbert slept downstairs. But there was an open ledge that Robbert used to store things, and when they put May in his bed he'd stacked those boxes and laid out a place to sleep. Instead of a staircase like Irene, he had a wooden ladder nailed to the wall. I had never climbed a ladder, but this was the last place the notebook could be, so I hurried to it and put my foot where I'd seen Robbert put his. The rungs were gritty with sand.

I pulled myself up, doing my best to grip the wide rungs, nearer to the whirring fans and less able to hear anything else. When my head came over the edge, I didn't see the notebook anywhere. But right in front of me, as if it had been hastily shoved there from the ladder, was a round shape, like a ball, covered with one of Robbert's white coats.

I climbed another step, enough to reach for the coat sleeve. I pulled. The ball underneath turned as the coat came free. From the sand I knew this was what Robbert and Irene had found on the beach that morning, and taken away before any of us could see.

It was someone's head.

I'd never seen a head quite like it, but I knew enough to recognize the shape, and the eyes and the mouth and what was left of the hair. The head stared right at me, even though something sharp had been shoved into both sockets and rattled around, like a knife getting the last bits from a can, leaving the socket edges broken and scratched. The mouth was dented with round welts, like from a hammer, and smeared with bright red paint, as if there were lips. There wasn't a nose, but I don't think it ever had one. The hair was mostly torn out. Only a few lank strands remained, revealing tiny holes where the rest had been woven through, now stubbled with uncoated wire. A tangle of cable trailed from of the neck, bedraggled with sand and kelp, like the tail of a jellyfish left by the tide.

There was more red paint on the forehead, symbols I didn't know, the lines just wide enough to be made with a finger.

I could only hear the fans. I didn't see the notebook. I had to go. There was nothing to do about the head except think, and I could think as I went. I wanted to know what her name had been, where she had lived, everything she'd known, but I knew

I'd never get a single answer. Before this, the only thing we were certain never to know was our parents. Was that what death meant—no answers, a finally locked door? As my foot touched the floor I decided that was wrong, because death always left a why, and a how, and a what next. Questions weren't the same as answers—they didn't tell me this dead girl's name—but for her sake I wasn't going to let them go.

I rushed down the steps to the courtyard, holding the rail. The rattling crack ripped through the air again, this time much closer, and a cloud of birds burst from the palms, frightened by the noise.

Halfway up the hill, I heard them call. I had almost fallen twice, trying to go too fast and slipping on the slick red dirt. I hadn't seen them, crouched in the rocks.

"*Where have you been*?" whispered May.

"Do you have the notebook?" asked Eleanor.

"Did you see Caroline?" asked Isobel.

Caroline wasn't with them. I looked behind me, down to both buildings and the courtyard. She wasn't anywhere.

"Where did she go?"

"To find you," said Isobel. "To find the notebook."

I shook my head. "She didn't come to find me. She went somewhere else. Didn't she say?"

"She just went," said May. "By the time we noticed she was halfway back."

"She said it would only be a minute," said Isobel.

"We've been waiting for you both," said Eleanor.

All three of them—the other two imitating May—were crouched in the rocks, and I realized I'd crouched down, too. I looked down the hill. How could Caroline be out of sight so quickly?

"We have to *go*," said May. "It's too late. Didn't you hear the shots?"

"You should keep going and hide," I said. "I'll find Caroline. Maybe by then Robbert and Irene will be back, too—"

"*No*."

May burst from the rocks. She grabbed my arm, spun me toward the hill.

"We're all *going*," she grunted, "and we're going *now*. You don't understand." She called ahead, still angry, to Eleanor and Isobel. *"Move!"*

They hurried in front of us, holding hands for better balance, while May pulled me after. There were more sounds behind us that I didn't know.

"What's all that?" I asked May.

She was too caught up with hauling me to reply. We were almost to where the path turned, the point beyond which someone standing in the courtyard couldn't see. I looked back. The kitchen blocked my view of the beach path, which was where the sounds echoed. They were *voices*—far away, speaking loudly, but with words I couldn't understand.

"It's people!" I said.

"Get down!"

May dropped to her knees, and I did my best to crouch with her. Isobel and Eleanor had stopped ahead of us. May furiously waved for them to keep going. She peeked back herself and either decided we'd come far enough to stand or that there wasn't enough time not to. We caught up with the others.

"What are they saying?" asked Isobel.

"Do you understand them, May?" asked Eleanor.

But May only let go of my arm and pushed to the front. Her face had changed, jaw stuck out and eyes all hard, like when she was angry, but I knew she was also scared, even mainly scared. This was how people were able to do things when they didn't want to—they made themselves feel something else, like anger, more than the fear. May must have learned it from her uncle, the way we learned deductions from Irene, which made me think of deducing what had happened to Caroline.

She'd woken from a dream where Robbert had said to take his notebook. I thought of my own dream, the only one I'd ever had: May's eyes and the round holes in the plank, and somehow knowing that May's past would tell me what had happened in the storm. Since Caroline's dreams weren't a random matter of sand so much as direct results of what Irene whispered before bedtime, or questions Robbert asked her when they were alone in the classroom, with time I could guess what the different connections were. But there was no time. I looked back. All I saw were rocks and palms and, higher and higher around us, the bright blue sky.

But if I couldn't deduce her dream, perhaps I could deduce Caroline's waking. She woke slowly after dreams: she'd said to find the notebook, but it wasn't until later that she knew I wasn't looking in the right place. But why didn't she come tell me, so we could look together? Because there wasn't time—which meant Caroline knew more than anyone what was wrong.

She had asked Irene not to send her to sleep.

Why did we know things when we did? When did the knowing settle in, like a circling bird to the earth? Caroline hadn't known what to do until she was on the path. But she hadn't gone back to the courtyard. She'd gone somewhere else.

"Robbert had the notebook with him," I said.

Isobel and Eleanor turned to me. "What?"

"That's what she knew from her dream."

We had stopped walking, which brought May rushing back to us. "What are you doing—come on!"

"Caroline went to find Robbert," I told her.

May just stared. Her voice was raspy, like when we'd found her.

"Then she's not coming,"

May led us higher than we'd ever been, near where Irene had placed the second tub of rice. Robbert's aerial stuck out above us, a pyramid of gray rods rising from a metal box bolted to the stone.

"It's there." May pointed down, beyond where we could see, into nowhere. "You have to be careful, but you can get there."

But we couldn't see it. We couldn't *think* it. We had never been so close to the edge, and May was pointing to go even closer.

"I don't think we can," said Eleanor.

"You have to. Watch me. Watch where I put my feet and hands."

But as soon as May began to clamber down, from behind us rose an echoing scatter of sounds—crashing and splitting, bangs and slams. We couldn't see where they came from. May scrambled back, and quickly up to the aerial for a better view. She came down even faster.

"What's happening?" I called.

"Is it Caroline?" asked Isobel.

"No! Watch me! Watch my feet!"

May made herself go slow so we could see, creeping farther out on a spur of rock. "One foot here, and then here . . . and then here—and your hands on this crack, one at a time. Don't look down, and it's just like going down steps." She stopped, her body hanging over the sky, right at the point where another step would take her around and out of sight. "Who's coming first?"

No one wanted to come first. We weighed differently than May, different amounts in different places. Our hands and feet didn't grip like hers—they weren't as soft. It was a very long way down, onto the rocks if the tide was out, into the water if it wasn't.

"Eleanor!" shouted May. "You're nearest—you first!"

"But we're not supposed to go near the edge!"

"I'll help you—don't worry."

May came back to the first step, holding on with just one hand and one foot, perched in the air, and reached to Eleanor. Eleanor came to the edge, extremely slow and careful.

"We're not supposed to do this, May."

"I know. But you have to."

"Are you sure?" asked Isobel.

"Yes!"

"But we don't know how," said Eleanor.

"I'll tell you. Face the rocks. Move sideways, like a crab. Put your first foot there."

Eleanor nodded, blinking. Thinking about crabs was a helpful suggestion, as long as you didn't fall. Not falling depended on strong arms and good balance. May could balance her whole body with one arm. I didn't think we could.

I tried to figure out how long it had taken to climb, and how soon anyone coming behind us might arrive. It could be any minute.

Eleanor's hand slipped, scraping moss off a rock she'd been trying to grip. May was right there, though, pressing a hand to Eleanor's waist before she tipped backward. Eleanor got a better angle on the rock and held tight.

"Are you okay?"

"Yes, May."

"Now step here." May lifted her foot, nodding that Eleanor should step where she'd been. Eleanor did, then slowly shifted her hands at May's direction. They were almost past the edge of the cliff, where we wouldn't see them. May craned her head around Eleanor and called. "I'll be right back for the next one!"

"It helps to think about crabs," called Eleanor, "and the rain trap."

They went around and we couldn't see them. Isobel and I both thought hard about the rain trap, remembering how Irene and Robbert had secured it to the roof. The canvas was too heavy to be held by anything but all the ties together. Since they could only attach one tie at a time, one of them did the attaching and the other kept the rest of the canvas in place with both hands. So whenever Eleanor lifted a hand or foot, she made sure the rest of her hands and feet could balance all her weight, and we would have to do the same.

Isobel pointed downhill. A plume of black smoke twisted up above the palm trees.

"What's being burned?"

I shook my head. It could be a lot of things.

"Pssst!" We turned to see May coming back.

"Is Eleanor in your cave?" I asked.

"Safe and sound. Who's next?"

Isobel was nearest, so she began to very cautiously step and grip in the exact places Eleanor had, with May's free hand hovering just in case. Watching Isobel made me think of grasshoppers in the morning, dew still heavy on their wings, long legs picking a cautious path from stalk to stalk.

"Watch your foot, that step is slippery," whispered May.

Isobel didn't answer, blinking rapidly, but made sure her foot was settled before she moved her hand. I watched how she had to wedge her feet, because ours didn't bend the same as May's. They reached the curve, and then inched from sight.

I stood alone. The black smoke had thickened. I heard new sounds, closer on the hill. Voices, getting louder. I had nowhere to go.

I had seen Eleanor and Isobel. I thought about the rain trap and crabs and picked my way to the first step of their path, careful not to lean my head too far forward. It would be easy to just go headfirst off the peak. I remembered learning to use stairs, how Irene and Robbert had knelt to catch us when we fell, and how many times we'd needed to be caught. But finally we went up and down without a hitch, though smart girls always used the rail. Next had come walking uphill and downhill, and after that walking on sand. Each time Irene and Robbert had been there to make sure things worked.

But, like all of us, I had been paying attention to why and how we improved.

I inched my way out, gripping into the angled crack above my head and shifting my feet from spot to spot. The open space fell wide below me. I could hear the waves. The tide was in, crashing and strong. Part of me wanted to know how far down it was, but it meant turning my head which meant changing balance. Instead I stared at the rock in front of my eyes—the tiny bubbles from lava, moss, white spatters from the birds. I squeezed with each hand and tilted my feet, leaning into the peak instead of outward.

Voices broke out behind me. Then a shout. More shouts, angry and sure.

May's face popped around the edge and almost knocked me

off. Her hand shot out and caught me, pressing my chest against the rock.

"Bloody hell—*what are you doing?*"

But May had heard the voices, too, because she was whispering. She looked past me, her eyes wide. The arm on my back shifted to my hand and guided it quickly to the next hold, then dropped to my foot and did the same. In three quick steps I was around the edge. I didn't see the cave. White waves smashed to foam on the black rocks below. I felt myself slipping, but May braced my leg. How much farther could I go?

"Right here," whispered May, then she hissed behind her. "Make room!"

May swung herself down and half her body disappeared. She reached back, guiding my foot to its next spot. She pointed to my hand.

"Hold on. We can catch you."

"I'm too heavy to catch. I can't see the cave."

But she did catch me, and I wasn't too heavy because the lip of the cave was right beneath my foot. May's hands brought me in and Isobel and Eleanor were there, too, crouched in the low overhang. May held a finger to her mouth. I crawled in from the edge and we all listened.

"Did they see me?" I whispered.

May waved me to silence. The cave faced the water and

the surf was loud. I couldn't hear anything from where we'd been.

From above us came another loud cracking rattle. Then smashing metal and even louder shouts. A blur of shadow fell past the cave, hurtling to the water. We pushed forward to look, but May held us back.

It was the aerial. Whoever had thrown it down would be peeking over the edge to watch it land, and if we looked out they would see us, too.

We waited. Was it only the aerial that had made them shout, or had they seen me, too? We couldn't run any farther if they tried to climb in.

I looked around the cave, wondering how May had ever found it. The rocks were still white from all the birds, but May had swept it mostly clean. In the back lay the blanket from Robbert's bed, next to May's own zipped bag, Irene's water jug, and a stack of plastic tubs.

Outside in the air the birds sailed past, gulls and terns, veering near but wheeling on when they saw their spots were taken.

We nearly didn't hear. It had been an hour since the aerial fell into the sea. We had whispered about what to do, but May said to wait for everything to stop. No one knew what stopping meant, but since we couldn't go back and forth to the cave like she could—we were lucky to have done it once—it was up to May to check things when she wanted, and right now she didn't.

She had just said she didn't—again—and all of us were quiet. May scraped at the floor with a jagged piece of rock, carving lines in the chalky white. I touched her hand to make her stop.

"Listen," I said.

It was a voice, thin and high. It was Caroline.

Eleanor touched May's arm. "You have to go!"

"What is it?" asked May, because she hadn't heard.

"It's Caroline," I said.

"You have to help her in!" said Isobel.

"Bloody hell," said May. "What if it's a trap?"

"It's Caroline!" said Eleanor.

"But how?" May shook her head. "How could she escape?"

"She did!" said Isobel.

"She must have hid like us," said Eleanor.

"I'll go help her," I said, trying to get past May. But May shoved me back and growled. She was out of the cave and clinging to the rocks before we knew it. I followed to the lip of the cave. May craned her head around the edge, toward the peak. I turned to Eleanor and Isobel. "Help me."

I put a hand where May had put hers, and then extended my foot into the air, feeling for the right stub of rock. I felt Isobel's palm against my back, helping me balance. May disappeared around the edge. She was talking, but I couldn't get the words. I inched along, Isobel having to reach so far to help me that Eleanor had to help her, too. I finally inched my head around. May was halfway back to the peak. Above her, right at the brink, tottered Caroline.

Robbert's satchel hung from her right shoulder, heavy with the notebook. Somehow she had found it and somehow she had found us, too. Her smock was torn and black with soot. Her smooth face had been scratched, the abrasions clogged with red dirt, looking like May's scab. Caroline's left arm hung limp, dangling from an inch of exposed cable at the shoulder socket.

She dipped her torso and the satchel slipped clear. Caroline caught the strap before the notebook hit the ground, and then held it out for May.

"You have to take it," she said. "He put everything inside to keep us safe."

"Caroline!" I called.

May whipped her head around. "What are you doing? Get back!"

I didn't care. "Caroline, what happened? Come with us— we're safe!"

"Take the notebook," Caroline said to May. "Robbert made sure I knew it was important. Please."

May hurried forward. "Give me a second! I need my hands free to help you climb."

May caught the satchel strap and ducked her head through the loop, making sure it fell against her chest so its weight wouldn't pull outward. She clambered into position and patted where Caroline needed to place her first foot.

"Come on now."

"But we're not supposed to go near the edge."

"That doesn't matter. It's all changed—come on now."

Caroline stepped near the edge, but she was weaving. Something had happened to her leg, too.

"Careful!" cried May. "One foot at a time . . ."

Caroline nodded, standing still. May looked back to me.

I heard Isobel and Eleanor from the cave.

"What's happening?"

"What's wrong?"

"She can't climb," hissed May.

"Caroline!" I called. "Where did you go? Where are Robbert and Irene?"

She turned to my voice, tottering again. It was her left leg, dimpled at the knee.

"I saw the fire. I watched them break it all. Smash the aerial. I fell down."

"Where are Robbert and Irene?"

"I don't know." She shook her head, as if those words were wrong. "I don't *understand*. I didn't see what to do."

"We couldn't do anything," I said.

The wind pulled at her hair like it pulled mine.

"Stay there," called May. "We can find another place for you to hide."

"There isn't one," said Caroline softly. "I looked."

She stood at the cliff's edge, blinking, trying with all her mind to answer all she'd seen.

"*May!*" I whispered, pleading.

May's fingers squeezed the rock. I saw how tired she was, the tears in her black eyes. She inched closer to Caroline, reaching out. "We can try. Look at me! Put your hand where I have mine."

But Caroline's eyes had swept past us, to the sky. Too late I realized her attention had been captured by the birds, soaring and diving around the peak. She stood in the center of a spinning globe, transfixed and taking refuge in the patterns.

"Caroline!"

Her head tipped back to follow a rising gull. In a terrible, silent instant her balance changed and the weight of her body turned on her weak leg. Then Caroline toppled out, straight off the edge and down. She struck the rocks halfway and bounced, spinning like a star, into the foaming sea.

11.

We stayed inside the cave until May's water jug was empty, almost three days. Then she told us to wait and climbed out alone. We sat together until May reappeared, peeking around the edge. She called to us: no one else was on the peak and she was going to take a look farther down. We wanted to come with her, because if anything happened to May we couldn't get out of the cave. But getting us all in the cave had been so difficult that it made sense to wait until we were completely sure of being safe before we went to all the risk and trouble. May promised to be careful and quick, and she was gone.

"Besides," said Eleanor, "if there is trouble, we'd be just as stuck out there as we'd be stuck in here without May."

"And May is good at sneaking," agreed Isobel.

Since we were good at learning, that was what we did while

we waited, thinking of everything that had happened so fast. It was what the three of us had been doing since we came to the cave.

We had also all taken naps, because a short nap every day kept our systems cycling clearly. May slept longer than we did, curled on her blanket in the back of the cave, but she stayed awake longer than we did, too, for more hours at a time. She spent a lot of time, while we talked and even while she talked with us, carving lines and shapes into the white dust. Sometimes we could tell what she carved—waves, boats, sun, trees—and other times we had to ask: a curve of lines was the wind, and a series of circles was sunlight. May also drew things that, when we asked what they where, only made her shrug. At first we thought she was carving secrets or even that she was still shy, but when we asked, May would shake head and tell us no, she was just drawing.

"But *what* are you drawing?" asked Isobel.

May shrugged. "I don't know."

"How can you draw without knowing what it is?" I asked her.

"How can you take a walk without knowing where it's going to end?" she answered.

"But that's not the same," I said. "A walk goes to the place it ends but it also goes to the places in between."

"Exactly," said May, scratching again with her sharp rock. Before

I could say I didn't think it was exactly anything, May stopped scratching and tapped the rock to get the dust off. "And just because I don't know *now* doesn't mean I won't know ever, either."

I almost understood—because we learned by adding one thing to another thing to make a third we hadn't known before—except May didn't add things like we did. She felt them, like the weight of an object in the dark of a pocket, hidden but still at hand.

That was May's everything. That was May's heart.

Eleanor had set the satchel on the blanket. May hadn't said anything about the satchel or the notebook it held, because she was too busy yelling at me for climbing out on my own and then at Isobel and Eleanor for helping. When she'd come back in the cave May had yelled and yelled, with tears on her face, about how it wasn't going to be her fault if we kept being so stupid. May pushed her way to the back of the cave and threw herself down on the blanket. We didn't know what to do. A minute later May surprised us all by saying she was sorry.

"For what, May?"

"For *her*. For not saving *her*."

"But you couldn't have saved her," I said. "Could you?"

May shook her head.

"Caroline's leg was damaged," I told the others. "And her arm. And her face. She was damaged all over."

"I shouldn't have let her get near the edge. Aren't you supposed to stay away from the edge?"

"You said all that changed," said Eleanor. "You were right."

"We have to deduce and make decisions," said Isobel.

"Caroline decided the notebook was more important than being careful," I said.

May shook her head. "Don't you care? Don't you care about *them*?"

"Of course," said Isobel.

"Maybe Irene and Robbert are hiding, too," said Eleanor.

"Maybe they are," said Isobel.

We waited for May to agree with us.

"They aren't," she whispered. "Believe me."

I remembered Caroline's words. Not that she didn't know, but that she couldn't *understand*.

I didn't understand her being gone, either. I had seen her fall. Now her part of any conversation would always be unsaid, and the direction she would have gone walking would always be empty. Her absence extended in lines of numbers made of smoke, backward in memory and forward in futures never to occur.

"Now there are only three of us," said Isobel. "We do still have to be careful."

I touched May's knee. "There are four."

But May only shut her eyes, which was her way to stop talking.

Though finding the notebook had cost Caroline her life, no one moved to take it from the satchel, much less turn it on and look inside. For Eleanor and Isobel, using the notebook for ourselves meant May was right, and Robbert and Irene were gone. But I remembered that finding the notebook had come from Caroline's dream—which made me think of how Caroline was different, and how I was different, too. I made my own decisions about time. I made decisions about May. Where the other girls, given an assignment, pursued a result, I had learned to see possibility.

So I pulled the notebook from the satchel and set it on my lap, where everyone could see. The keys were made for more—and thinner—fingers, but I could still make it work, one touch at a time. While the notebook powered up, Eleanor took everything else from the satchel and spread them out, like we'd spread the things from May's bag: Robbert's crumpled shirt, two pencils, a plastic sharpener, an empty case for his glasses, a scrap of cotton he used as a handkerchief, the notebook's charging rod, and a little flat wallet. Eleanor unzipped the wallet and folded it open. Each side held a row of metal rods, with different tools at either end.

"Look," said Isobel, pointing to one of the tools.

She extended her arm to show the tiny crescent-shaped spot in the crook of her elbow—in all our elbows. The tool's tip was perfectly shaped to fit.

"What else is inside there?" asked May.

"The three of us," I said. "And all we're made of."

But once the notebook came alight, nothing was different from how it always looked—certainly there was no new note that told us what to do. The little windows that tracked weather and sea currents had frozen, because they depended on satellites and needed the aerial, but nothing else had changed. I saw the same large archives, one for each of us, and partitions for the many different subjects, like cognition or syntax or energy, that went beyond any one girl. But none of that was new, none of it *now*.

"Is there a message?" asked Isobel. "Does it say when they'll find us?"

I shook my head but still began to open the archives, though I didn't know what I hoped to find. The others stared closely at the screen, and even May scooted nearer to look over my shoulder, but all I found was what we knew was there: diagrams, numbers, diaries, pictures, charts. After a few minutes May leaned back on the blanket. The rest of us searched on without saying a word, for hours, until the sun began to set. At last I darkened the screen and returned the notebook to Eleanor, who slid it gently into the satchel.

One of the three of us always kept awake in the cave for our hearing. But it turned out there was nothing to hear—no voices, no whispering, no more crashing or loud bangs. Only the waves below and the squawking birds. We came to recognize their different calls pretty quickly, until we could tell which birds were around the cave or wanting to come in—because they did still think of the cave as theirs—without having to see them. We asked May if any birds had come in, when she'd been in the cave alone. She said she'd found a few one morning, but that as soon as she sat up they'd been scared away. She imitated herself sitting and then raised both arms at once, making a loud flapping sound like an explosion of wings and feathers. May laughed out loud and made the sound again.

"That was the last of those birds. They'll think twice for a long while. Especially if they think I'm *hungry*. Because I'm a lot bigger than they are!"

"Robbert and Irene never ate birds," said Eleanor.

"Do you eat birds on a boat?" asked Isobel.

"Hell no," said May. "Too many feathers, no meat, and you'd have to cook 'em forever. And you can't cook *here* at all."

"I'm sorry there's no more rice," I said, because May had eaten the rest of the rice our first night in the cave.

May shrugged. We sat for a moment, and May's stomach started to make noises. No one said anything, because we had heard those noises before, but May slapped her stomach each time and told it to be quiet. Then she laughed in the back of her throat. "Maybe I'll try seagull after all."

Aside from naps, we found other ways to divide the time. Since my incident with sand I was extra cautious about all the dust in the cave. May wrinkled her nose and shrugged, but I explained that the smell was less important than the particles in the air being small. Eleanor volunteered her smock, so we untied it and asked May to use it to wipe the dust from our bodies, and especially our hair. May wiped us each twice a day and said it was just like waxing the deck of the *Mary*, except without the wax. Once we wiped off the dust, each of us sat with our hair in the sun for at least an hour, taking special care because that meant sitting near the edge. Since we could each go many days without sunlight, this was less about survival than being responsible with our time. But we all agreed that schedules and survival went together.

Taking care of the dust was the first cooperation we had all done since May had helped us into the cave, but we ended up being able to help her, too, even though it took a lot of explaining on her part. When she'd lived in the cave by herself, May had been able to climb back onto the peak and use a nook in the rocks for her toilet, even though it wasn't a chemical toilet like Robbert and Irene had behind the kitchen. But when she tried to climb out now we all wanted to know why, and even when she explained we all agreed it was too dangerous, so we worked out a way for us to hold her arms while she squatted over the edge of the cave. When she was done we pulled her in. We were all very curious about what she was doing—questions Irene had never been interested in answering. May wasn't any different, except to say it was always easier on the boat for Will and Cat, but she wouldn't explain why that was either.

May wouldn't explain a lot of things, just like she didn't want to talk about what had happened that last day. Whenever we turned to her for answers she would only shrug. But three days is a long time to hide your thoughts and eventually May did talk, or at least stopped trying not to listen. I watched how her face changed, especially when we talked about our parents, because what had happened to them could help us understand what had happened on our island.

But what I realized most by watching May was what it meant, even if she came from a different, bigger world, that she'd spent almost all of it on her boat. The more we wondered about the angry people who'd swept like a storm across our island, the more I saw—in what May didn't know, either—that her uncle

Will had made his own rules for being careful, which had kept May out of sight, especially when they met other boats or stopped in port, especially ports with schools that might have taken May away. It was just like how Robbert and Irene, we now realized, had hidden us—from the supply boat, from the rest of a changing world.

That was when I remembered the head. I had set it to the side in my thinking, but when we recalled that last morning and our walk on the beach with Irene—to the very moment when we'd seen the boat—we saw what we'd all forgotten: the trail of Irene's and Robbert's footsteps, that earlier in the morning they'd found something important enough to make them go back right away.

When I told them what I'd found in the classroom, Isobel and Eleanor had my same questions. Who was it? What had happened to her? What did the red paint mean? When May didn't ask any questions I asked if she could answer ours. She shook her head. I asked if she'd ever seen anyone else like the head— like us—ever before. She shook her head again.

"That's why May was so surprised to see *us*," said Isobel. She made me describe the head again, especially all the differences— the shape, the color, the differing style of hair, the mouth.

"Who could have been *her* parents?" asked Eleanor.

We couldn't know. May shifted, tugging at the blanket.

"There are stories," she said.

"Stories of what?" asked Isobel.

"About—" She stopped and found another word. "About girls like you. People tell them in towns. On the wire."

"So you *did* know about girls like us," said Isobel. "Then why did you scream?"

"I didn't know anything," said May. "I'd only heard, but hearing isn't real—and everyone knows not to trust it. And nothing like that—like you—is tolerated, not any more, not in any towns. Will didn't like any talk about it, especially not me, because that gets you seen, and we lived quiet."

We waited for her to say more. May shook her head.

"But once . . . once there was a boat that left Port Orange." May wiped her nose on the back of her hand, and then the hand on her shorts. "That's all I know."

But it wasn't. We waited for her to go on and she finally did. "Will traded with them. He and Cat went over and I watched. It kept outside the harbor, just like us—and big, with a dish, and weapons—rockets, and that's business. When Will and Cat came back I asked what it was like, and they said not to worry, they'd made a good trade. I wanted to know about the boat, how big it was, what it *did*. Cat said they made things. Will told him to be quiet. I never knew what Cat meant, but maybe now I do. That was the last time we went to Port Orange. Someone saw us trading and we had to scoot."

"What is scoot?" asked Eleanor.

"We had to *go*."

"Where is the big boat now?" asked Isobel. "Did that girl fall off it?"

"She must have," I said, "because she washed up. But that doesn't explain the paint."

No one spoke. While the others might have been thinking of paint, I thought of how rarely Irene ever showed us what she felt.

They had found the head. They saw what had happened to that girl and knew what might happen to us. It must have made them sad and angry and scared, but all we had seen was Irene with her same smile and same voice waking us up and going for a normal walk. And if the boat hadn't come, what would she have said about their footsteps coming to a stop? Would Robbert have buried the head like he buried the plank, to preserve our ignorance?

I looked at May, crouched with her knees up to her chin, my story weaving through her thoughts just like her story weaved through mine. Did her silence reflect an Irene I'd never known?

When May came back the rest of us were ready.

"I looked all around," said May. "I think it's safe."

"Did you find Irene?" asked Eleanor. "Did you find Robbert?"

But May only wanted to know who was coming first, telling everyone else how to help and how to be careful and how we could see everything for ourselves when we were finished.

I went last, as I had been the last to arrive, waiting alone in the cave while May made a special trip with the satchel and blanket and the plastic tubs. The birds glided past outside, waiting to get their cave back.

"Come on," May said, swinging into view. "My arms are wobbly."

But she was smiling, a tired smile on a dusty face. I followed every direction until I was around the curve, clinging to the rock with May's free hand to brace me. Isobel and Eleanor waited on the peak, well back from the edge, and waved when I appeared.

"Don't wave back," grunted May.

I tried to say that of course I wouldn't, but she just told me to put my hand *there*. Soon I was next to the others, watching May pull herself to safe ground. She slapped the grit from her hands and sighed.

"That's enough of *that*."

The rocks above us were scratched where the aerial had been torn from its perch and dragged down. May began to walk, but the three of us stayed where we were.

"There's nothing to see," May called. "Come on."

But we had to look. To be careful we held hands and took small steps toward the edge. The tide was out, so the black rocks were exposed, hard and sharp, but May was right. I picked out the jagged spur where Caroline had struck halfway down and where she would have landed, searching for even the smallest sign. There was nothing. The waves had taken every part of her away.

"Come *on*," called May, and she started down.

The high grass had been flattened on either side of the path, and we passed spots where it was burnt. I remembered the column of smoke, which was like listening to Irene, when we could predict her whole sentence just by the first few words. The burnt grass and the memory of smoke were the same first hints of what we knew we'd find below.

We stopped in the meadow.

"O no!" cried Isobel. All three of us were blinking. "O no!" cried Eleanor and I together.

That the sky was vast and blue made what we saw so clear, and all the normal sounds of the island seemed like an acceptance of what had happened. Was everything this temporary?

"We're lucky the fire didn't catch across the whole island," said May. "I don't think they cared—they just piled things on and let it go."

In the center of the courtyard lay a great burned heap of ruined things. It looked like everything from both buildings had been hauled into a pile and set on fire. What hadn't been burned outright lay twisted and blistered and melted and black, and covered in ash.

"They used fuel." May wrinkled her nose. "You can smell it."

To get all the machines outside, the classroom had been knocked to pieces. Because of the big cells on the roof, more fuel had been poured on the floor and set alight. A lot of what made our buildings didn't burn very well, but even so the classroom now reminded me of the dead girl's head. The head itself had disappeared. It must have been thrown on the pile.

The kitchen looked almost as bad—the door was smashed and the windows kicked in, though it still had walls and a roof.

We walked down to the courtyard. Gray ash rose in puffs around our feet. We just stared, blinking. Each place we looked only showed another thing gone.

"There's a lot of work," muttered May.

"We need to take naps," said Eleanor. "We need a safe place from storms."

"I know," said May. "There's a lot to do."

"But it's destroyed," said Isobel. "We can't live in the cave. We *can't*."

May left us, all staring at the burned pile, and climbed onto the kitchen porch, stepping carefully.

"Don't hurt your feet, May!" I cried.

May held out a hand which meant she wanted us to watch. She bent over and lifted a corner of one of the windowpanes—a wide square of scuffed plastic—sliding the rubbish on top of it into a pile. She held the window high for us to see, May herself an opaque shape behind the plastic, because of the scuffs and soot.

"See?" she called. "It isn't broken, just knocked out of the frame."

She shook the plastic between her hands, so it made a noise. May set it down and her face had a grim sort of smile.

"We can put it back. We can take care of ourselves."

"How?" asked Isobel.

"Just like that." May waved at the kitchen. "It's more broken than destroyed. We can fix it up. Come on."

May heaved the broken railings off the steps to clear a path for us to climb. We studied the size of the plastic square and the broken window and saw that she was right.

"It will take nails," said Eleanor.

"Or glue, or ties," said May. "But look at the door—same thing. Handle's gone, but we don't need a handle."

We turned our attention to the broken door, already thinking about what spots didn't fit anymore, all of us crowding around. May picked her way inside and shouted to follow. Again, at first it seemed like only debris, but May kept pointing out the difference between tipped over and actually ruined. The machines had been pulled out, and the stove. But May squatted under the cupboards and called out that the pipes and wires were all still in the wall. She stood again, with her hands on her hips.

"On a boat you fix things."

We stood where the kitchen table had been—it was tipped against the wall with two legs snapped off—trying to see the difference between how it had been, and how it was, and what was possible.

"But this is a house," said Isobel. "Do you know how?"

May nodded. We waited for her to say more. We needed to know. When she spoke May's voice was soft.

"Will told me. It was a night when Cat was sad, after too much drink. Will knew I had heard Cat being sad, and he came down to my bunk and told me something to remember." May tossed the hair out of her eyes. "He told me that one day he'd be gone."

"And he is gone," said Eleanor.

May nodded. "But he told me not to be sad."

We knew that May *had* been sad, that she was sad now from her shining eyes, but no one said so, because we knew May knew it, too. She let her breath out.

"He told me to remember what was good. He said it would make me sad—he said it was how much you loved things that made you saddest—but that I should remember him anyway.

Then he talked about that very day, which wasn't special, but he told me about it like I hadn't even been there, like a story. And in the story I saw *us*. Us. I saw our lives."

I looked at the littered floor and noticed the metal knob on a drawer that had been smashed to pieces. With both hands I pulled the knob free.

"What are you doing?" asked Isobel.

"We *do* need a handle," I said, "because our hands are different. But we don't need the same one as before."

The knob ended in a metal screw that seemed as big as the hole left in door. I stuck it in and felt the sharp tip catch. May came over to help and held the door, so I pinched hard and turned the knob, four times. When I let go it stayed in place. May let the door swing shut and opened it again, using the new handle. Then Eleanor and Isobel each tried it for themselves, pulling the door open and pushing it closed.

"A different handle works very well," said Eleanor, blinking.

"Wait!" I went to Robbert's satchel, which May had set down to pick up the window. I carried it back inside and Eleanor and Isobel used their flattened hands to clear a space on the countertop. I set the notebook where everyone could see.

"Is there a message after all?" asked Isobel. "Did you remember something we didn't see?"

I shook my head. "Nothing new is in the notebook. Now is

what's new, and how we have to think. We have to find different handles. But the notebook can tell what handles there are to choose from. *Look*."

I opened one of the oldest file archives, whose name hadn't meant anything: *haven*. Inside were more diagrams and designs, lists and pictures, all about the two buildings where we'd lived, showing everything about how they were made, and out of what, and why.

"The files show what fits together," I said. "Everything left over from the classroom, or what didn't melt in the fire. Wood and pipe and wire. Even if they didn't go together on purpose, we can find what *fits*."

"A handle is anything," said Isobel. "Like cage and parrot."

"A handle is anything," echoed Eleanor.

I knew May couldn't read the words, so I opened another file archive, the one named energy.

"That's about us," said Isobel, pointing to an icon of the four of us standing in the sun.

"But also Robbert's roof cells. And the cooker and the kettle."

"And the lights?" asked Eleanor.

"And the lights," I told her. "And all of it together, down to the smallest part."

"Down to the thinking," said May.

"Is thinking small?" asked Isobel.

"Small as air." May tapped my head with her finger. "And just as big."

We began where we were in the ruined kitchen, picking things up as we talked, setting what wasn't broken after all off to the side, and going back and forth to look in the notebook to compare what we'd found to its files. May helped move the bigger pieces and wriggled to places and corners we couldn't easily reach. The stairs to Irene's room were smashed, but May still clambered up and called back that the roof was still whole, that we'd be safe from the rain.

We were collecting pieces of our cots when I realized May had gone outside. When I called her name and she didn't answer I hurried onto the porch, the others crowding after me. How long had she been gone? Had something happened to her? Should we go look? But then I saw her coming up the beach path, carrying a bucket made from a yellow nylon bag that slopped water as she walked. She set it down on a step, right next to a stack of coconuts we hadn't seen her collect. I looked into the bag and saw it held a dozen colored shells. May crouched to look with me and poked her finger at one of the shells, which spit a stream of bubbles. The others came up to look for themselves.

"Tons to eat in the tide pools," May said. "I'll make a fire later.

And the rain barrel's good, too, tipped over but doesn't leak."

"There are more planks on the beach, May." Eleanor pointed. "We found them on the rocks. We can reuse them."

"That's the idea," said May. "We can reuse it all."

But the moment of missing May had taken my thoughts somewhere else. May noticed I wasn't looking at the shells. She stood up.

"We have to make sure, May."

"I know we do." May sighed. "Come on, then."

The four of us climbed down the kitchen steps—careful because the rail was gone—and walked to the dock. The red dirt path looked no different. Only the planks of the dock showed any sign. The metal cleats had been torn out, and the dock was scraped and scarred across its tar-stained surface, the gouges almost writing, as indecipherable as the voices we had heard on the peak.

I remembered watching Irene scale a fish Robbert had caught, the rough passage of her knife that pulled the fish skin tight and stripped it clean. Was that what had happened to the dock? Was that what had happened to us?

Of Irene or Robbert we never found a thing.

Only afterward, sorting through the mess, could we attach them to objects: Irene's teacup, whole in a heap of smashed dishes, a hair clip, the little tub of sweet wax for her lips, canvas shoes. Since the classroom had been burned, we had less of Robbert, only what had been in the satchel. We wiped ourselves with the handkerchief and hung his shirt, once it was clean, next to Irene's blue dress, for May to wear whenever they might fit.

The rest of that first day was filled with work we never imagined doing. We gave up living one now after the next, and turned our days to make tomorrow. That was the only way to fix things before rain, cook food before dark, and make sure everyone stayed safe.

At night we sat in a line on the steps. The stars rolled past above us, bright stitches on a deep dark blanket. Determined to remember everything, we sang.

ACKNOWLEDGMENTS

This book began as a libretto for an opera, many years ago. My thanks to Liz Duffy Adams, Michelle Andelman, Shannon Dailey, Madeleine George, *Joe* on 23rd, Joseph Goodrich, Markus Hoffman, Todd London, Honor Molloy, Suki O'Kane, Julie Strauss-Gabel, Nova Ren Suma, Anne Washburn, Mark Worthington, and Margaret Young.